PALE AS A GHOST

STEPHEN OSBORNE

Dreamspinner Press

Published by
Dreamspinner Press
4760 Preston Road
Suite 244-149
Frisco, TX 75034
http://www.dreamspinnerpress.com/

Pale as a Ghost

Cover Art by Anne Cain   annecain.art@gmail.com
Cover Design by Mara McKennen

ISBN: 978-1-61581-836-5

Printed in the United States of America
First Edition
April 2011

eBook edition available
eBook ISBN: 978-1-61581-837-2

To Matt Downing—a good if unlikely friend

and

Traci Bridget—the best cheerleader a writer could have.

CHAPTER 1

THE bullet hit the brick wall behind me, taking a nice little chip out of the masonry and missing my left ear by mere inches.

The shooter, a middle-aged man with a receding hairline and bad teeth, shouted, "Come on out, Andrews! I promise not to hurt you!"

I wondered how stupid he thought I was. After all, trusting a man who just fired several shots at you isn't something that comes easily to most people, myself included. I stayed nicely hidden behind my Dumpster and yelled back, "No, thanks! I'm fine here, thank you very much."

He fired another shot, which struck the wall again, much further away. I was lucky the guy was such a lousy shot. I pulled my own gun, a .38, from my belt. I really didn't want to shoot the man, but who knew if he might get lucky after a while? I peered around the edge of the Dumpster. The alley was full of shadows, but I could see his silhouette about halfway down. He was just standing there, not even attempting to protect himself. I know he was angry and desperate, but surely he should have taken into consideration the possibility that I might be armed as well. After all, I was what is commonly referred to as a private detective. They often, at least in novels and the kind of TV movies shown on the USA Network, go out armed. Granted, the guy wasn't thinking straight, but still.

The man shooting at me, one Barton Clifts, was a mid-level management guy who worked for a pharmaceutical firm. Barton had siphoned off around $70,000 from the business, and I had been called in to investigate. I found the proof, and he was supposed to have been turned over to the police. However, he somehow eluded capture and had come looking for me. Apparently he blamed me for all of his problems. It wasn't my fault that he made discovering his embezzling so goddamn easy. Some people just don't use their brains. But then, he wasn't the guy hiding behind a Dumpster.

"Come on out, Andrews," he called again.

"He certainly is persistent," a familiar voice said. Seconds later I was joined behind the Dumpster by my boyfriend, Robbie Church. As usual, Robbie just seemed to appear out of the ether. One second there was a shadow; the next he was there, accompanied by a slight chill in the air. He was wearing an Everlast T-shirt and black basketball shorts. He liked to dress casually whenever possible. Also, as usual, he looked like he was all of twenty years old, which continually annoyed me. I hated that I had aged ten years, and he had stayed the same. "You must have done something to piss him off, Duncan."

"I caught him embezzling from his company. I think he's mad at me."

Robbie took a quick peek over the top of the Dumpster. A shot rang out, and Robbie quickly ducked back down. "He's not exactly a marksman," he said with a smile.

"Why are you ducking?" I asked. "Afraid he'll kill you all over again?"

Robbie grinned. "He may not even have seen me. Most likely he was just taking a potshot. Even if he was gifted with the ability to see ghosts, I doubt in his present frame of mind he'd be able to. Not everyone has the focus you do, luckily for me."

Great. I was getting Ghost Lessons 101 from my deceased boyfriend. "Why don't you go and haunt somebody else," I suggested, "and leave me to get on with my work."

He pointed to the gun in my hand. "Why don't you just shoot the asshole? He's standing right out in the open."

"I was about to do just that when you popped up. You've been in this alley before?" Ghosts, as I learned long ago, can only appear in locations they'd been to in life. The alley was in the old warehouse district on the east part of the downtown area. I couldn't imagine why Robbie would ever have ventured to such a place.

"Apparently," he said. "Not that I remember, but I might have wandered down here after a concert or some late-night binge. I must have been lost." He looked at the end of the alley, which was blocked by a large wooden fence. "This alley doesn't really go anywhere."

"I noticed that when he started shooting at me, and I ran down here for cover." Another shot winged by. "I don't suppose you could help out here, could you?"

Robbie frowned. "Why don't you just shoot the mother and get this over with?"

"You know I don't like to use a gun unless it's absolutely necessary."

Robbie popped his head up and a bullet went right through where his forehead would have been had he been corporeal. It might just as well have gone through mist for all the effect it had on Robbie. "This might be one of those times."

"That warehouse behind him must have been made into apartments at one time. I noticed a window a few floors up that had a potted plant on the window sill. He's right underneath it, if you get my drift."

"You know how hard it is for me to move objects," Robbie said with a roll of his eyes. "Really. Just shoot the guy already. He's getting on my nerves."

I looked into those deep brown eyes that I'd fallen in love with all those years ago. "Please," I said. "Do it for me."

Robbie sighed and disappeared in an instant. I carefully peeked around the corner of the Dumpster and saw that Clifts had actually moved forward a little. He was now illuminated by the lamp post at the end of the alley. Several floors above him Robbie appeared, sitting on the window sill with his legs dangling. The flower pot was next to him. I saw him draw in as much energy as he could and give the pot a push.

The terracotta pot hit the pavement a good three yards behind Clifts. It did, however, cause the man to start violently and turn around. "Shit," I muttered as I quickly took aim and shot him in the leg. Clifts let out a yell and clutched at the wound with his free hand. He turned and fired wildly in my direction. I breathed in and shot him in the arm. Luckily for him I'm a good shot. It didn't hurt that he really wasn't that far away. The man fell, screaming in pain.

Robbie appeared at my side as I rose from behind my protective covering. "I missed," he said. He looked somewhat paler from the energy he'd used pushing the pot.

"Yeah, thanks. I had noticed." I pulled out my cell phone and was about to call 911 when I heard sirens approaching. Someone had heard the shots and had already called. I looked at Robbie, who was starting to look transparent and more like what people think ghosts look like. "You'd better get out of here. I really don't want to explain to the cops that my boyfriend who's been dead for ten years still hangs around."

A moan came from the alley where Clifts was laying. We ignored him.

"Like they'd be able to see me anyway," Robbie said, a little petulantly. "Honestly, sometimes I think you don't like having me around."

I sighed. For a dead guy, Robbie had a lot of self-esteem issues. "You know I love you, and I always will."

I could see by his face, pale as it was, that he wasn't convinced. "What were you doing in this part of town anyway?"

"I was going to Sam's Place for a drink." I knew he wouldn't like the answer, but the sirens were coming closer, and I wanted to get rid of him quickly.

"You were hoping to pick up someone." Robbie folded his arms and turned his head away from me. "Some boyfriend you are."

A patrol car skidded to a halt at the end of the alley. "We'll have to talk about this later, okay? Why don't you get back to the apartment and check on Daisy?" Daisy was my beloved bulldog, who had some problems of her own—the main one being that she, too, was no longer alive. However, she wasn't a ghost like Robbie. Daisy was a zombie. Long story.

"At least she still loves me," Robbie pouted. He vanished just as several policemen began scanning the alley with their flashlights. I put my arms up so they would know I wasn't a threat. "Over here," I called to them.

It would be a long night explaining the chain of events. It would have been longer, though, if I also had to explain Robbie the ghost boyfriend to the cops.

CHAPTER 2

I'M NOT psychic, which is what most people assume once they know that I can see ghosts. I can't read minds. I can't even read palms. Come to think of it, I have a hard time understanding my phone bill. No, I was merely born with the Gift, which makes me sensitive to paranormal phenomena. Lots of people have it in one form or another. Some don't have it at all, and if a ghost was standing right in front of them, they wouldn't see it. Some people born with the Gift lose it over time because they convince themselves that their eyes are playing tricks on them. After all, there are no such things as ghosts, right? Some have the Gift so strongly that they not only can see ghosts but can sense other paranormal creatures, such as vampires or demons. Oh yes, vampires exist. Always have, as far as I know. So do demons, zombies, witches, warlocks, and goblins. It's a fun old world, if you only open up your eyes and your mind.

Robbie and I originally met at a party up in Lafayette. He'd just graduated from high school, and I was finishing up my studies at IUPUI (which stands for Indiana University/Purdue University at Indianapolis, in case you were wondering). A few minutes into our conversation we discovered that not only did we both live on the west side of Indianapolis, but we even lived within a few blocks of each other. This ended up being a good thing as when we left the party, Robbie's car refused to start, and I ended up giving him a ride. It was on the sixty mile trip home that we bonded over our love of science fiction television shows and a deep, abiding passion for the Mel Brooks movie *Young Frankenstein*. By the time we pulled into his apartment complex, we were fast friends. The differences—he was a jock, I was a geek; I was a voracious reader, he only read Spider-man comics, etc.—didn't seem to matter. Neither did the few years age difference. We soon became lovers and found that we matched each other perfectly in bed as well. As soon as his lease was up, he moved in with me.

At that time I was renting a small house not far from campus. When I'd signed the lease, I was surprised that the house had been empty for so long, since it was perfect for students, and the rent was very reasonable. I soon learned the reason. A horrible murder had taken place there in the 1950s, and the house was reputed to be haunted. My first week there I found the reputation was well-earned. The ghost of a forlorn-looking young man walked the halls and would occasionally creep into my bedroom to tickle my feet in the night. I never learned why he enjoyed this activity. The spirit, I discovered, was named Sam, and he had been murdered by his girlfriend. She had been unreasonably jealous over one of his co-workers and had ended up shooting poor Sam in the head.

A few days after he'd moved in, I related the tale of the haunting to Robbie, leaving out the part about my contact with the ghost. Robbie found the prospect of living in a haunted house exciting. "Have you ever seen anything?" he asked.

I knew I could trust Robbie, but I still hesitated. I didn't want to come off as a raving lunatic. Finally trust won out, and I told him about Sam and the tickling. "I've always had an affinity with ghosts and the supernatural," I told him. "Growing up, it almost seemed like ghosts sought me out to tell me their woes. It got me into a bit of trouble because I thought that everyone talked to ghosts. When I got to school, everyone thought I was a loony."

I could tell Robbie was skeptical but anxious to find some proof that Sam really existed.

We soon learned that Robbie was unable to see Sam, although he would often catch sight of a shadow out of the corner of his eye. When he turned there would be nothing there. Robbie often felt cold spots in the house, though, and woke up several times feeling that his feet had just been tickled. On several occasions he'd walk into the kitchen to find every cabinet door open. Objects often went missing for days, only to show up in a totally different part of the house. Before long, Robbie was a firm believer.

We never knew what caused the fire that burned our little house to the ground. The fire department put it down to faulty electrical wiring, but I wasn't so sure. In the days prior to the blaze I'd catch sight of Sam, looking sadder than ever, fiddling with the stove or other appliances. My guess was that he was unable to move on while the house was still standing. After the fire, I never saw or heard from Sam again. If Sam was some sort of arsonist spirit, at least he picked a night when Robbie and I were at the movies. Got to give him credit for that.

With most of our belongings now ashes, Robbie and I began apartment hunting. After we found one (the apartment I still call home), we decided to get a dog to cheer ourselves up. At that time Daisy was just a normal, exuberant little bulldog. Things changed for her a few years ago, but I'll go into that later.

The new apartment was spirit free, something that made Robbie and me a little sad. We had gotten used to dealing with Sam and his problems. By this time I had graduated from college and was working for a large detective agency. Robbie delivered pizzas. We were annoyingly happy.

Then one night a van full of drunken teenagers rammed into Robbie's car. He was killed instantly.

My grief was profound and lasted up to the day of his funeral—which Robbie attended. I was sitting in the front pew, crying my eyes out, when I noticed a drop in temperature around me. Before I could react Robbie was sitting next to me, wearing the suit he was about to be buried in. He looked around him with a mischievous little smile.

"Good turnout," he said.

As there were no screams or people rushing to the exits, I assumed I was the only one who knew he was there. I lowered my head and whispered, "What the hell are you doing here?"

He rolled his eyes. "That's gratitude for you! I come back to keep you from crying incessantly, and you give me attitude. You know I can't stand to be away from you for long."

I have to give him credit. The tears stopped. It was too difficult to deal with Robbie being at his own funeral service and cry at the same time. I said between clenched teeth, "You need to get out of here. What if someone here manages to see you?"

Robbie shrugged as the minister strode up to the podium and gazed out at the mourners. It seemed to me that he paused a second as his eyes passed over the spot where Robbie was sitting, but that may have been my own paranoia. The minister cleared his throat loudly. "It's always tragic when a life is ended too soon, and the life of Robert Randall Church certainly ended much too soon."

"You're telling me," Robbie said. "Now I'll never be anything except a pizza delivery guy. I won't get to find out what career I would have had! And by the way," he leaned in to me and continued, "the accident was *so* not my fault. That van came out of nowhere. They must have been going at least eighty miles an hour when they rammed me."

"Ssshhh!" I hissed.

Robbie paid no attention to me. As the minister continued with the eulogy, Robbie kept up a running commentary. He actually was pretty funny. By the end he had me smiling.

He's been with me ever since.

CHAPTER 3

I DON'T have a real office. My detective agency is run through a virtual office. It's all e-mail and websites and answering machines. There is an actual office building, up on the north side of town, and that's what's listed as the address on my business cards, but I don't technically have an office there. When I have to meet with a potential client, I arrange for a small meeting room at the office building. It saves paying for an office that I would rarely use.

There are downsides to this arrangement. For one, when I meet with a client it's usually in a bare, utilitarian room with no personality. I also don't get to have a waiting room complete with secretary, like Sam Spade had. Of course, I wouldn't have a leggy blonde for a secretary. Or if I did, it would be a male leggy blond. Robbie would probably get jealous, though, and find some way to scare the shit out of him. Still, I often yearned for an actual office where I could put pictures of... well, Robbie when he was still alive and Daisy before she became a zombie. Robbie had been quite a looker, despite a somewhat large and broken nose, and Daisy was adorable. She still was if you overlooked the slightly gray tinge to her fur and the bloodshot eyes and her penchant for eating squirrels and rats in a rather disgusting manner. You get that with zombie dogs, though.

I didn't bring Daisy with me to meet with Janice Sanderson. I found that clients didn't appreciate the presence of a strange-looking bulldog. There was no chance of Robbie appearing, either, as he'd never been in the office building.

The room contained a bare desk, which I sat behind. Janice sat on the other side. She was in her early forties, although she wasn't the sort to admit it. Her dark brown hair was pulled tightly back, and she wore a no-nonsense business suit of a dull green. She probably thought she looked like Rosalind Russell in some old movie. If smoking had been allowed, she'd have lit up.

"I want you to find my daughter," she said. She even had the quick snap to her voice. If I'd looked like Humphrey Bogart, she'd have been happier. But hell, Bogart would have had an office of his own.

I nodded. I thought about doing my Bogart impression and saying that the police had a whole department devoted to missing persons, but I wanted the case. Private detectives have to eat too. "How long has she been missing?"

"Two weeks. I'm guessing as to the time. It could have been longer. It's been two weeks since I've heard from her and none of her friends have seen her in that time." She crossed her legs rather demurely. I wondered if she knew the action was wasted on me. I raised my eyebrows just a fraction to make her happy. She was a potential client, after all.

"Have the police been informed?"

She frowned at me. Bogart wouldn't have asked that question. "They are under the impression that she's run away with one of her boyfriends." Here she looked down so she didn't have to look me in the eyes. "She's not been herself lately. She's going through one of her phases. She'll do anything to annoy me."

"Like running off with a boyfriend?"

That got me an angry glare. Janice Sanderson bit her lip and decided to ignore my comment. "Brenda just turned twenty. She doesn't live at home any longer, but she does keep in touch. Kevin, that's my son, and she are very close. Kevin still lives at home. I'm sure that's why she still comes around. It's certainly not for me."

"Does she live alone?" I asked.

Janice shook her head. "She has a roommate. This girl, Tiffany, and she live downtown. I don't believe for a moment that Tiffany is her real name. Even Brenda is using another name nowadays. She calls herself Amber."

Tiffany. Amber. I took a stab in the dark. "Where has Brenda been working?"

Janice sighed heavily. "She's been working at one of those clubs; this one is called Pickin's. Imagine, my daughter a stripper! She's just doing it to annoy me." Mrs. Sanderson uncrossed her legs. Maybe she noticed it wasn't getting her anywhere. Janice obviously liked to be noticed. Someone should tell her that the green business suit wasn't helping. However, the diamonds in her earrings were nice.

For the next half-hour, Janice Sanderson filled me in on lots of little details of her daughter's life, or at least what she knew. It was enough to get started at any rate. A missing person case isn't easy for a one-man operation, but I told Mrs. Sanderson I'd do what I could. When she left she actually batted her eyes at me and told me she looked forward to seeing me again. Some people just don't pick up on signals.

HE SHUFFLED across to the refrigerator, feeling less human than he had in quite a few years. It was time. He knew this, more by his internal clock than by the calendar that was affixed to the wall in his kitchen by a thumbtack. The man looked at his hands. He could see the aging process beginning. Fine lines and wrinkles showed on the back of his hand. He knew that if he went to the bathroom and checked the mirror there, he would no longer look youthful and fit. He'd have aged, looking decades older. Just yesterday someone had guessed his age at twenty-three. Now he'd be doing well if he could pass for his mid-forties.

The flesh would rectify all that.

Opening the refrigerator door, he looked at the meager offerings inside. *Nothing looked good. Even the raw beef didn't sound appealing. Eating it would only leave him wanting. He needed the flesh. The man closed the door and glanced over at the counter where his knife rack sat. The large butcher knife, which stood out amid the smaller cutlery, seemed to be calling for him. Yes, it was time.*

CHAPTER 4

DAISY met me at the door when I got to my apartment. She barked excitedly, and I leaned down to scratch her ears. Her tail wagged appreciatively. "Who's a good dog?" I asked. She didn't answer, but she did blink her bloodshot eyes. Even zombie dogs like attention.

I could sense Robbie's presence in the apartment even though he was nowhere in sight. Just floating around the ether, I figured. I called out anyway. "I'm home!"

He didn't reply. Probably still sulking. Well, screw him. He'd been dead for ten years after all. Surely I could at least hook up with someone for some casual sex without Robbie getting all mopey on me. It wasn't like I was getting any from him. I had just sat down on the couch and had grabbed the TV remote when my cell phone rang. I fished it out of my pocket and answered. It was Gina, my best friend.

"Darling," she said, "we have to go out somewhere to dinner tonight. I have some absolutely fantastic news!"

"Sure," I said. "Where do you want to go?"

She named a restaurant, and I had to immediately nix the idea. Robbie and I had been there. I needed a Robbie-free night. "Let's try somewhere new," I suggested.

Gina named a Mexican place that had only recently opened downtown. I tried to think of other restaurants that had been in the same building that Robbie might have gone to. I couldn't. "That sounds fine," I told her. "Give me an hour or so, though. I've got to take Daisy to the park so she can catch a squirrel for dinner." Not for the first time I found myself wishing they made Purina Zombie Dog Chow. It would be easier, but I knew it wouldn't work anyway. Zombies have to have living flesh or nothing. It's just a zombie thing.

When I arrived at the restaurant I found Gina already there, dressed as usual in a long skirt and voluminous shirt with lots of frills. Gina would fit in any local opera production as a Gypsy extra. With all her rings and earrings, "Gypsy" was a word that fit Gina well, although "witch" was more accurate. Gina wasn't the New Age sort of witch, either. Not a Wiccan. She was a spell-casting, honest-to-goodness witch. It had been she who, years ago, had resurrected Daisy when she'd passed away. It had seemed like a good idea at the time.

I sat down, and Gina smiled at me. "You've got a new client," she said.

"You've been looking into your crystal ball," I said.

Gina shrugged. "Don't need a crystal ball to see that you're feeling prosperous. Your aura has changed."

Our waiter was a thin, redheaded kid who seemed to think that flirting with me would get him a bigger tip. He was right, of course. He wasn't even the age Robbie had been when a car accident had ended his life. When you're over thirty, you can't help but like it when someone under twenty flirts with you. I can't, anyway. Gina and I ordered, and the waiter flittered off, promising to check back with us in a few minutes.

"So what's your news?" I asked, sipping my water. Gina's face split into a grin. "I'm dating someone!"

"Really?" I tried not to feel jealous. "Human, or…?"

"He's human. His name's Mark. He's a dentist."

A witch dating a dentist.

"I think this was a sitcom back in the 1960s. Does he know you're…?"

"Of course not! It's not something you bring up right away. 'Would you like to go out on a date?' 'Sure, but I'd better tell you first that I'm a witch.'"

"There's the age difference to consider too. You were around at the Salem witch trials."

Gina scrunched her face. "That's witchist. Whenever anyone wants to point out that a witch is old, they always reference Salem. I was around long before that, and you know it."

"Fair dues. Most people don't have a witch as a best friend."

Gina shrugged again. "You're different than most people. You were born special. You can see more than most. You know of the things that lurk in the dark. That's what makes you such a good friend. You don't judge or have preconceived notions."

"I've got a dog that eats live rats, and I'm haunted by my dead boyfriend. I can't afford to be too judgmental."

The waiter brought our chips and salsa. "Need anything else to drink?" he asked, giving me the tiniest of winks. "Your entrees should be out shortly."

"We're fine, thanks," I told him. He shimmered off.

Gina scooped a good amount of salsa onto a tortilla chip and chomped on it. "I thought you'd be happy for me," she said.

"I am." I tried the chips myself. They were nice and salty, just like I liked them. "It's just that... I'm wanting to start dating myself." I saw Gina's eyes bug out. "I don't mean dating *myself*. I've been doing that for ten years now. It's gotten to the point where I buy my left hand chocolates on Valentine's Day. What I mean is that I want to start dating other people."

"I thought for a moment there," Gina said, wiping a bit of salsa off her lip, "that you were going to ask me to conjure up a doppelganger for you. Don't look so shocked. A lot of people have fantasies about having sex with a double of themselves."

"I'd settle for another human being, preferably male. And good-looking. I'm not picky. Johnny Depp will do nicely."

Gina helped herself to more chips. "What does Robbie think of this idea?"

"He's pissed off at me right now. He just doesn't understand that I need… well, the touch of another man. Plus, Robbie still looks like he's twenty."

"That's the age he was when he died," Gina reminded me unnecessarily.

"Yeah, but I look thirty. Because I am. Robbie is always going to look twenty, and I'm going to keep getting older and older. It's going to look very strange at some point."

Gina blinked. "Like having a dead boyfriend still around isn't strange enough."

"You know what I mean. Plus, there's the no-sex factor. It's okay for Robbie. He's dead. Apparently things change once you've breathed your last. Me, I'm still horny."

I hadn't noticed that the waiter had come back with our food. He heard my last statement and smiled at me. "I get off at ten, honey," he said. "Maybe we can take care of that little situation."

Gina waited until he'd departed once again to chide me. "You didn't take him up on his offer."

"He's a baby. He probably just graduated from high school."

"That's the good thing about the young. You can teach them things. Besides, I don't think he was offering you a long-term relationship. He was merely suggesting a brief fling."

"He probably lives at home still, and we'd have to go back to my apartment. And what would happen then? Oh yes, the ghost of my old boyfriend would appear and find some way to scare the piss out of him."

"You're going to have to talk with Robbie and arrange something," Gina said, digging into her food, "or you're going to stay celibate for the rest of your life."

I frowned. "My love life doesn't stand...." I let the sentence trail off.

"What?"

"I almost said a ghost of a chance, but I swear I didn't mean it as a pun."

CHAPTER 5

I FIRST met Gina the day after Robbie died. I had spent the day with his parents, making arrangements and drinking a little too much wine with his mother. Ma Church could sure put away the Merlot. She also brought out old photo albums of Robbie, which I could have done without. I held my tears until I got to my car, and then the floodgates opened.

I don't know how I ended up at Gina's little cottage. It certainly wasn't on my route home. Maybe karma brought me there, or, as Robbie had termed it, my Spidey-sense. I saw her sign advertising Tarot readings, though, and went inside. I didn't really want a Tarot reading. I didn't really know what I wanted. Probably just someone to talk to.

When Gina answered the door, I saw her enveloped by a green aura, and I knew she was someone special. She was prepared to give her customary greeting but stopped when she caught sight of me.

"You are one of the special ones," she said.

"Yeah," I replied, "well, right now I'm not feeling all that special. And it may be the Merlot playing tricks on me, but do you always have the green glow around you?"

We ended up talking all night.

Gina didn't tell me right away that she was a witch. It's not something that comes into conversation easily. In fact, I was to find that Gina revealed very little of herself. The few facts I came to know about her I learned over time, as every now and then she'd let something slip out.

Stereotypically, women have an aversion to revealing their true age. Gina certainly does. I know that she's at least a couple of hundred years old and had indeed been at the Salem Witch Trials, but as a spectator and not as a participant. She also mentioned that several times she had given Tarot readings to Mary Todd Lincoln. "I warned her that her husband would face danger at some sort of entertainment. She took it to mean that they should stay away from fairs and traveling shows."

Her dating life was in many ways worse than mine. A man she lived with in the 1920s discovered that she was a witch and set fire to the bed she was sleeping in. The flames utterly destroyed her. She remained in a sort of limbo—details as to what she meant by this remained sketchy at best—until 1968. At that time her little cottage was occupied by a small group of hippies who thought that it would be groovy to use one of the spell books they found tucked away in the attic. They attempted a conjuring spell and ended up resurrecting Gina. She shared the house with the hippies for several years after that. "It seemed only right, as they thought the house theirs, and they had brought me back to life. They were quite nice, really," Gina once told me. "Although they were a tad nervous around me. I think they thought that if they stepped out of line I'd turn them into a newt or something."

The hippies eventually moved on, and Gina stayed on in the house alone. She never lived with anyone after that and, until the dentist, had never dated anyone to my knowledge. An ex burning you to death can sour your whole attitude toward dating.

Gina's powers, despite the fears of the hippies, did not extend to actually transforming someone into a newt. She could give you a nasty wart or the worst case of zits you've ever seen, though. Gina could foretell the future (not her own or mine, not with any accuracy anyway) and was a master at spells and potions. Love potions were a specialty of hers, but she always warned me against them. "Unless you're very careful they can go horribly wrong. Plus they're very hard spells to break and nearly everyone wants to break them eventually. People are so fickle."

When Daisy got hit by a car, Gina took me at my word when I said that I couldn't live without her. She cast one of her most ambitious spells, and the results were surprising to say the least. I never had the heart to tell her she may have misinterpreted my meaning.

I couldn't complain, though. Gina once used Daisy to track me when I'd been knocked unconscious. She cast a spell on the dog, allowing the animal to pick up my scent even though I was miles away at the time. Good thing, too, as I was badly concussed. I would have died had they not found me when they did.

So all in all there were good points to having a dead boyfriend who was still around, a zombie dog, and a witch for a best friend.

CHAPTER 6

AT TEN o'clock the next morning, I had another interview with a potential client. Two in two days. Wow. I might actually get the rent paid on time if this kept up. The client, who had sounded very nervous over the phone, was one Ellen Boyd. She was very vague about what she needed to see me about, preferring to tell me in person.

Ellen Boyd turned out to be in her early thirties and would have been very pretty except for the circles under her eyes. She sat across the desk from me and tried to smile. It wasn't a successful attempt. She wore black slacks and a red blouse. Her fingers drummed on the arm of her chair. "A friend of mine recommended you," she said. She was having a hard time looking at anything but the edge of the desk. "Penny Van Orten. You helped her find a missing necklace."

I remembered. It had been fairly easy to find, since it had been stolen by her teenage son, who had intended to pawn it. The whole case had taken only a couple of hours of my time. I also found the Van Orten house to be haunted by the ghost of a previous owner. Penny Van Orten had actually been hoping that the ghost had mischievously hidden the necklace, not wanting to believe her precious son to be guilty. The fact that I could see the spirit inhabiting their home had impressed Mrs. Van Orten. "I remember her," I said.

Ellen Boyd bit her lip before continuing. "Penny said that you knew things, could see things, that other people can't. She said you had an ability to communicate with…." She stopped. "God, this is so hard."

"She told you I can see ghosts," I said helpfully.

That got me a smile. "I never believed such things existed before a few months ago. Tanner—that's my husband—and the girls had been watching some scary movies one night. I was out with some friends. I never would have let the girls watch such trash myself. If I'd known…."

The air conditioning kicked on, causing her to jump. She composed herself and looked me in the eye for the first time. "I shouldn't be bothering you with this," she said, gathering her purse closer to her as if she was ready to leave. "You're a private detective, not a ghost hunter."

"I'm a bit of both. Relax, Mrs. Boyd. I've dealt with all sorts of things. There isn't anything you can say that will shock me."

She settled back into the chair. "Apparently in one of the movies some of the characters used a Ouija board to talk with a ghost. The girls thought this was a wonderful idea and wanted to use one. We don't have a Ouija board, but Tanner cut out pieces of paper and lettered them, and then he carved a planchette out of a piece of wood."

"He made his own spirit board."

Ellen Boyd nodded. "Nothing happened. The three of them just had fun frightening each other. I was so mad when I got home and found out what Tanner had done. You hear all the time of how dangerous Ouija boards are. Tanner just laughed. He didn't believe in ghosts, you see, so he thought it couldn't do any harm."

"And you?"

She frowned, confused. "And me what?"

"Do you believe in ghosts?"

"I didn't before," she admitted. "Strange things started happening after that, though. Little things at first. Lights on when I'd known we'd shut them off. Cabinets and drawers opening seemingly on their own. And then one night I saw her."

"Her?"

Ellen Boyd brushed some of her long brunette strands off her face. "I was home alone. It was a couple of weeks after the little session with the spirit board. The girls were at soccer practice. Tanner was going to pick them up after he got off from work. It had just started to get dark, so it must have been about eight o'clock. I walked into the kitchen and there was a woman standing by the stove. She wasn't entirely solid. I could see her, but I could also see through her. She sort of glowed blue."

"Did she seem to notice you? Make any attempt to communicate?"

Ellen looked surprised that I wasn't laughing at her story. "No. She just stood there for a second and then vanished."

"Have you seen her since?"

She nodded. "Several times. Always just for a brief moment. Tanner thinks I'm seeing things. He also thinks I'm just forgetting to close the drawers and such. The lights coming on, he puts down to faulty wiring. The girls haven't seen the woman, either. They do think that something is going on, though. They've had items moved from their rooms only to show up in different parts of the house. Annie, that's my youngest, has also heard what she describes as weird moaning late at night."

"But your husband has had no experiences?"

Smiling softly, Ellen Boyd replied, "That's what he says. But he's just a little too forced in his denial, if you know what I mean. Like he can't get himself to admit to things he's seen."

I nodded. "And what would you like me to do?"

She shook her head. "I'm not sure. Prove to me that I'm not crazy. Get rid of it."

"There are several ghost hunting groups in the area. They can come in with their equipment and do an investigation. You don't need a private detective for that. As for getting rid of the spirit, I'm sure you could find a priest willing to perform an exorcism on the house."

There was something in her eyes, a nagging qualm that she was reluctant to voice. Ellen leaned forward in her chair, rubbing her hands over her chin and mouth in indecision. She blew out a lungful of air and sat back. "I've seen this woman before. Somewhere. I can't remember where. Alive, I mean. She just... looked familiar. I described her to Tanner, and I swear he went pale. He said the description didn't mean anything to him, but I could tell it did. Tanner knows who it is."

"What did she look like?"

"She looked to be quite young, maybe in her late twenties. Kind of pretty, although that was hard to really tell, since she was blue, and I only have seen her for a few seconds at a time. She was tall, or at least several inches taller than me. She was wearing modern clothes. I mean, it wasn't like she was in some Victorian gown. Just slacks and a blouse."

I sighed. I hated to turn down work, but I also had to be honest with Ellen Boyd. "My services aren't cheap. Like I said, you could find a ghost hunting group that will do the investigation for free, and—"

"I need to find out who she is," Ellen Boyd blurted out. Realizing she'd spoken with more force than she'd meant, she regarded me sheepishly. "I'm sorry, but I know my husband is hiding something, and this... this ghost has something to do with that. I guess that's why I came to you. I need you to find the connection between this woman and Tanner."

I nodded. I figured that Ellen was probably reading too much into the situation. After all, suddenly sharing your home with a spirit can make one a little paranoid. Still, it should be easy for me to learn the identity of this mysterious ghost. I doubted if it would interfere with the Sanderson case, and who was I to turn down some extra money?

I looked over at a wall calendar the office building thoughtfully provided. It featured little kitties. Today was Tuesday. "I can come by

Thursday night and check the house out, if you like. I'd like to have your husband there if it can be arranged, but it might be for the best if your daughters aren't. Is there somewhere they can go for an evening?"

"My mother can watch them," Ellen answered. She looked happier now that I'd agreed to take her case.

I just hoped she'd look as happy when it was all over.

TONIGHT. The message seemed to be coursing through his veins. It was time. He couldn't wait any longer. He needed the flesh.

It had been so long, but he could still recall the taste. The taste of life. There was more to it than just replenishing himself, though. He enjoyed the killing. He enjoyed cutting into their bodies and feeling the life leave them. He liked the look of shock on their faces when they realized that they were witnessing their last few moments on this earth. He liked the feel of the knife as he plunged it into the soft flesh.

The man sat down in his living room on a wooden chair by the window. Outside there was little to see. A squirrel was making its way across the lawn to the big oak tree. The squirrel was flesh, of course, but the man had no interest in it. Surely such a small creature would not satisfy the mystical forces that enabled the man to live. Without thinking he found that his right hand had reached up to his chest to ensure that the amulet was there, that it was safe. It was. He could feel the worn wood beneath his shirt. He knew that the magic inside the amulet was damaged and that, maybe, there would come a day when it would no longer work. It would no longer allow him to be a man. Would he then revert to what he was, or would he simply die when the magic was all used up? He didn't know. Maybe he didn't care. Some of the symbols carved onto the wood were so worn now that if he hadn't known what they were supposed to represent, he would have no idea what they were.

At one time he'd thought about trying to re-carve the amulet, to make those symbols stand out again. He didn't have the ability, but he could find someone who did. Maybe he could find a witch to carve the symbols into the wood. Maybe a witch would give the amulet even more magic, enabling the man to live even longer. Maybe he wouldn't start to age after that, and he could just live forever as a young, vibrant man who had no taste for the flesh.

The man laughed. Witches had all but destroyed his kind. He would never find one who would work on the amulet. He just had to accept that the magic was flawed, and that every now and then he would feel the need for the flesh again. That was okay. He liked the flesh.

The man stood. The knife was calling. It was time.

CHAPTER 7

I HAD some time to kill—hours, actually—before heading out to speak to the night crew at Pickin's, so I made arrangements with Janice to check out Brenda's old bedroom at the Sanderson house. It had been months since Brenda had actually lived there, so I wasn't expecting to find any huge clues, such as a note from her saying something like "Hi! I've run off to Reno with Marty Smith from down the street!" One could always hope, though. Since Janice Sanderson hadn't changed Brenda's room, at the very least I should be able to get some idea of her personality from her belongings.

The Sandersons lived on what's known as the near-north side of Meridian Street. The houses there are uniformly huge and have lawns on which one could land a plane. The Sanderson domicile was a rambling, two-story structure with a small tower on one side going up a further floor. Even accounting for dens, studies, libraries or what have you, the house had to have at least five or six bedrooms. With Brenda gone, this left a hell of a lot of space for Ma Sanderson and little brother Kevin. Mr. Sanderson had run off with his secretary some three years ago. If Kevin had lots of friends over, they could play hide and seek and not find each other until graduation.

I worried if I had enough fuel to get my car down the long driveway. I did, although I felt sorry for the poor sap who had to tend to the Sanderson lawn. I couldn't see Janice out mowing the lawn in her business suit. I parked and went to the front door and knocked.

After a long pause the door was opened by a kid with long blond hair and a sour look. I assumed this was Brenda's adoring brother, Kevin. Kevin, judging from his long face, was not having a good day. Maybe he really was close to his sister and missed her. Or maybe he'd just lost at *Halo.*

"Is your mother in?" I asked.

He nodded. The kid looked so morose I wanted to buy him a puppy. Jerking a thumb he said, "She's in the living room."

Following the thumb, I came upon a cavern posing as a living room. The kid trundled upstairs, probably to practice for his *Up With People* audition. Janice Sanderson was seated on a long white couch right under a huge picture window. Her suit today was a dull gray. She had been leafing through *The National Review* but tossed it aside when I entered. "Mr. Andrews," she said as if in surprise. As I'd called not more than an hour before to set this up, the surprise sounded false. She stood and offered me her hand. With the grandeur of the room influencing me, I wasn't sure if I was supposed to shake the hand or kiss it. I shook.

"Thanks for letting me see Brenda's room," I said. I didn't take a seat. I hadn't been offered one, but the furniture really wasn't the sit-on-it sort. I'd have felt like a museum piece. I bet Kevin wasn't allowed to eat chocolate bars on the white couch. No wonder the kid looked glum.

"If you don't mind, I'll have Kevin show you her room. I have a few phone calls I need to make." Janice smiled thinly.

Yeah, I could see how swamped she'd been when I'd entered. An article in the magazine must have reminded her of needed work. I thought of Kevin upstairs. Goodness knew how far away the kid was by now. The house was big enough it could have taken up two zip codes. How the two communicated in the massive house without use of cell phones, or at least an intercom system, was beyond me. I calculated how long it would take to get Kevin back downstairs and nixed the idea. "That's okay. If you can tell me the way, I'll find it."

I did, although I was worried about not having a map. I thought about leaving a trail of bread crumbs to find my way back. No wonder

Brenda had bolted. You could have twenty people living in the house and still feel lonely.

Okay, actually it wasn't that bad. Brenda's room was just at the top of the stairs, first door on the left. Still, it was too big a place for two people to live in.

Brenda's room looked like a maid had just serviced it, as did the rest of the house. I hadn't seen any servants but there at least had to be a housekeeper. The thought of Janice Sanderson shoving a vacuum cleaner over the carpets was almost as comical as her behind a lawn mower. The bed was neatly made and even had a little pillow set on the covers between the two regular pillows. I looked. There wasn't a tiny chocolate placed there. I'd have fired the housekeeper. No wonder Brenda left.

The room had the bed, two closets, a dresser, a desk, and an entertainment center complete with stereo, DVD player, and television set for perfect viewing from the bed. There was a bookcase, but it was filled with DVDs. No books. I checked out the movie selection. Brenda favored teen comedies, Adam Sandler pictures, and the bloodier variety of horror movies. I had seen only one of the movies in her collection, and I'd hated it.

I turned on the computer on the desk. Her desktop picture was a photo of her and Kevin. Brenda was hugging the boy tightly, and he was hamming it up. Despite his stuck out tongue you could see he genuinely had affection for his older sister. There wasn't much on her desktop. I clicked open her iTunes. Most of the music listed was bands I didn't know, but it all seemed to be pop rock. Apparently Brenda was a longtime Hanson fan. She had everything they'd done since their first album. I hadn't even known they were still around. Hell, the little kids from the videos I remembered on MTV would be in their twenties now. It hadn't seemed like "MMMBop" was all that long ago. I turned off the computer, feeling old.

I was going through the dresser drawers when I realized I was being watched. I turned to find Kevin standing in the doorway, trying not to look curious. I smiled at him, and he gave me a nod.

"You're a private detective?" he asked. I guessed he was around fourteen or fifteen, and with his long blond hair he could have been in Hanson, if they hadn't aged.

I shut the drawer I was working on, not having found anything anyway. "I am," I admitted.

"And you're going to find my sister?"

I nodded. "She didn't tell you anything that would help me out, did she? Like where she went? Because if she did and you told me, this would be one of the shortest cases I've ever handled."

The kid cracked a smile. Morose teenagers loved my sense of humor. "No," he said, "she didn't tell me where she was going."

"She moved out a couple of months ago, right?"

"Beginning of summer. Moved over on the west side with a friend of hers."

"Have you been to her apartment?" While the kid was in a talkative mood, it seemed a waste not to ask a few questions.

"Once. Just for a bit before we went out for some burgers. Her roommate seemed nice. Really big boobs, but nice." From his tone I could tell Kevin couldn't care less about boobs, big or otherwise. I wondered if Janice knew that not only did she have a daughter who was a stripper but also a son who was a gay-in-waiting.

"Did Brenda have any special boyfriend? Some guy she hung around a lot?"

The kid bit his lip in thought. "Maybe the guy we had lunch with. Derek."

"What was Derek like?"

"Nice guy. Kind of dumb, but nice. Had some tattoos on his arms. A pretty cool cross. He was pretty muscular." Muscular was a major turn on for Kevin. He almost licked his lips when he said the words. I could see a future twink in front of me who liked rough sex. Go, Kevin.

"What did you guys talk about during lunch?"

He shrugged. "Movies. Cartoons. Cars."

"Does Brenda talk about Derek much?"

"She doesn't really talk about boys with me," he replied, sounding a little disappointed.

"When did you talk with her last?"

"It's been at least three weeks. Usually she calls me at least once a week."

"And she didn't give you any indication that she was leaving or anything the last time you talked to her?"

"No. Everything seemed normal. She was talking about getting a tattoo and how Mom would go apeshit if she did. We laughed."

"What do you think has happened to her?"

The slight smile faded, and he returned to the glum Kevin. "Seriously? I think she's dead."

"What makes you think that?"

"She hasn't called me. If she could, she'd call."

I hoped the kid was wrong. A funeral would only make him more depressed, if such a thing was possible, and Ma Sanderson might not have a black suit to wear.

CHAPTER 8

I KNOW of several private detectives who would love the chance to visit Pickin's and be able to add it to the expense account. I wasn't one of them. I hadn't been in a strip joint since college, when I'd grudgingly gone to one for a buddy's bachelor party.

I paid the cover at the door and thought about asking for a receipt. The brawny guy taking the money didn't look like he had much of a sense of humor, so I didn't. I wasn't armed, and I never was much of a fighter, and getting the crap beat out of me by a behemoth in a tight black AC/DC T-shirt wasn't on my list of things to do.

Inside, the place was as seedy as I expected. There were two stages, the main one along the back wall and another smaller one off to the side. These were just for show or maybe for special performances, since no one was currently dancing on them. The dancing was all done on the long, horseshoe-shaped bar. There were three girls strutting their stuff. It was early, and the crowd was thin, and most of them seemed more interested in drinking beer than watching the dancers. Maybe the leering crowd came later in the evening, or maybe it took several beers before the leering commenced. Either way, I felt a little embarrassed for the girls, dancing their hearts out with no one paying attention.

I found a stool and sat down. The bartender, who could have been a brother to the hulk who took my money at the door, came over and asked what I wanted. I ordered a gin and tonic. Not far from me a young woman with enormous breasts, wearing only a G-string, was gyrating to the music. She was looking my way, a little hopefully, I thought. I gave her a smile.

The bartender set my drink in front of me. I transferred the smile to him. I don't think he noticed. "Things are a bit slow this early in the evening, aren't they?" I asked. Great conversation-starter, me. He grunted and started to move away. I raised my voice a little. "Does a girl named Brenda Sanderson work here?"

The bartender stopped moving and turned back to glare at me. "Who wants to know?"

"Me. She went to high school with my little brother." I put my best innocent face on. I have a great innocent face. Some people have described it as vacuous, but that's just jealousy.

Brawny the bartender shrugged. "She works here. Or did. Haven't seen her for weeks."

"Aw, damn," I said with a sad shake of the head. "My brother really wanted to get in touch with her too. He's getting married. Would any of the girls know where she's gone?"

"If they did, they'd tell me. And they haven't." Brawny was very sure of himself. With biceps like his, I didn't blame him. He went off to wait on another patron. The dancing girl edged my way. I drank half of my gin and tonic in one go.

"You looking for Amber?"

The speaker was a guy in his early twenties with long, unwashed light-brown hair. He had crooked teeth with one missing in front. He was sitting on the stool to my left. I hadn't really given him much of a look when I'd sat down. I gave him more of an appraisal. He would be kind of cute if he cleaned up a bit and got his teeth fixed. "Her real name is Brenda Sanderson," I said.

He shrugged. "Amber to me. She's roommates with my sister."

"Think I could talk to your sister? It's really important to my brother to get in touch with Brenda."

Nodding to the dancing girl close to me, he said, "That's Tiffany there. That's my sister."

Oh yeah. Because it isn't creepy going to a strip joint and watching your own sister cavort about in a G-string. I suddenly needed to towel off my mind. I looked at Tiffany and then at Brawny the bartender. I didn't think he'd appreciate me questioning one of the girls during working hours. "Think I could have a word with her later?"

The guy nodded and offered to shake hands. "I'm Craig."

"Duncan Andrews," I said as we shook.

Craig's eye got a little twinkle. "You don't seem like the type of guy who usually comes into a place like this."

It must have been my handshake. I'd have to work on butching it up. "Not really, no."

He smiled at me and picked up his drink. "Let's move over to a corner. The music's not so loud over there, and we can chat without shouting."

Craig found us a small table at the far end of the place. He was right. One could almost talk in a normal tone and be heard there. Craig was wearing a tight ribbed shirt and even tighter jeans. I noticed as we sat down that he had a tattoo of a dagger dripping blood on his right forearm. He had a habit of shaking his head every now and then to get the stringy brown hair out of his eyes. "So what's a guy like you doing here?"

I indicated my half-empty drink. "I'd heard the gin was particularly good here."

Snorting, Craig replied, "You heard wrong. Do you really have a brother looking for Amber?"

"I have a brother. He lives in Rockford, Illinois and has a dairy farm. He's never heard of Brenda Sanderson, or Amber, in his life."

"So what's your real reason for wanting to talk to her?"

"Would you believe I'm a private detective, and I've been hired to find her?" By the look on his face I wondered if I'd have to resort to the old Don Adams routine and add some more. Would you believe I'm a Boy Scout, and I need my Missing Persons Badge? Would you believe I'm in training to join Scooby and the gang in the Mystery Machine? Eventually Craig's frown cleared, and he decided to believe me.

"You're gay, though, right?" Craig asked.

Usually at this point Robbie would have shown up. If the person in question wasn't able to see him, as most weren't, he'd have spilled their drink into their lap or something of that nature. As Robbie had died before the legal drinking age in Indiana, most bars were safe from his presence. Craig's beer wasn't going to take a tumble. "Yeah, I am. And here I thought I was so straight-acting."

Craig shifted in his chair so that his knee made contact with mine. He left it there. I don't know why, but I didn't move mine. Hell, it was contact with a male human being. "My sister won't get off until three in the morning," he said. "We can go back to my place and fool around until she's off work if you want."

I actually had to think about it. It had been an awfully long time, so long in fact that I was nearly ready to overlook the missing tooth. Maybe I could talk him into a shower before we got naked, and we could get his hair washed. The hair and the total lack of any romance won out. "Maybe some other time," I said.

Craig didn't seem fazed by the rejection. He did give it one last try, though. "I've got a really big cock. You look like you could use a good fuck."

Geesh, did it show? *Hair*, I told myself. *Bad teeth*. And I found myself thinking of Robbie. *Damn his hide*. "Another time," I said.

Craig and I ended up chatting for the next several hours. We had more than a few drinks while we talked. The bar had filled up nicely in the meantime and the girls were finally getting attention. I looked around every now and then and saw lap dances, lots of laughing and drinking, and hundreds of bills being stuffed into G-strings. A fun time was being had by all, it seemed. I was even getting to like Craig, in a weird sort of way. Then again, I was getting a little drunk. I switched to drinking Diet Pepsi once I realized this. I was, after all, on the job.

Eventually three o'clock rolled around. It seemed to take forever. A disembodied voice announced last call over the loudspeaker and people began to filter out. By this time Craig was swaying about a bit and slurring his words when he talked. Alcohol also had the effect of making him hornier, which was getting to be a problem.

"We'd better wait outside," he said, pronouncing "outside" as "oushide." "It'll take a while for Tiff to change her clothes, and they don't like people hanging around after they close."

We went outside. I had to help Craig walk and keep upright. The night air revived him a bit but only made him more of a handful. He kept trying to grab hold of my nipples through my shirt. I guided him to his car, which was parked in the rear parking lot. There were only a few cars remaining here and most seemed to belong to people who worked at Pickin's. The clientele who remained were quickly departing.

Craig sat behind the wheel and became all hands. He tried to kiss me. I turned my head. When he gave up trying to suck my face, he unzipped his fly and then tried to pull my head down. I resisted. It was like being in a small car with an amorous octopus. An amorous octopus with bad teeth and hair. "We've got time for you to suck my dick," he assured me. "You know how long women are getting ready."

I was beginning to wonder if waiting to talk to Tiffany had been the right thing to do. "I'm not really in the mood," I told Craig. And then the air changed.

There was a sudden rush of positive ions in the air, like after a thunderstorm. As there hadn't been a storm, I knew some sort of paranormal activity was either happening or about to happen in the area. I smacked Craig's hands away. "Quiet," I told him as I scanned the parking lot.

I could see one of the show girls leaving by a back entrance. She looked a little different with clothes on, but she had been the dancer who had been nearest to me when I'd been at the bar. She wore jeans and had a light jacket on, which she held closed at the front with one hand rather than zipping it up. She didn't look our way but headed along the side of the building and went down an alleyway.

"Where is she going?" I asked.

It was a rhetorical question, but Craig answered anyway. "That's Bethany. She lives just a few blocks away. She almost always walks home." Craig leaned in, trying to kiss me.

I got out of his car quickly and told him, "Stay here." My Spidey-sense was kicking into overdrive, and I knew something horrible was about to happen to Bethany unless I did something to prevent it. I shut the door on a surprised-looking Craig and started after her down the alley, wishing I had my gun with me. I was even wishing that Robbie had at one time blundered down that alley so he could assist me. Even the company of Daisy the Zombie Dog would have been a comfort.

The alley was dark, and when I entered I couldn't see much of anything other than shadows. There didn't seem to be any movement ahead of me, and I figured that Bethany had already turned a corner. I started to run, hoping I would catch sight of her at the end of the alley.

Her scream pierced the air before I got there.

CHAPTER 9

BETHANY'S second scream cut off abruptly. I got to the end of the alley and followed the sound. I saw two figures in the darkness ahead of me, down another alley that ran behind some houses. A dark figure was bending over Bethany's body. I couldn't see what he was doing to her, but I knew it wasn't good.

"Hey," I shouted.

The figure looked up, and I heard him snarl something. Lights from one of the houses gave a little illumination, but not much. He seemed to be dressed all in black and had what appeared to be some sort of hat on his head. I couldn't see his face. It was only by sixth sense that I knew the figure was male. He turned and ran.

I paused to look down when I got to where Bethany lay sprawled on the gravel. She was dead. Extremely dead. The guy had sliced her up with some sort of knife. A nasty gash on her neck and a huge slice across her abdomen were all I took in before I took off after the man. There wasn't anything I could do for Bethany now except catch the guy that killed her. I didn't know how I was going to do this since he was armed at least with a knife, and all I had in my pockets was my car keys and a tin of Altoids. Maybe I could mint him to death and key his car.

Ahead of me, the man vaulted over a chain-link fence into a yard. He landed perfectly and kept running. I reached the fence several seconds after him and didn't have his luck or skill. My leg got caught on the top of the fence, and I tumbled over the other side in a heap, ripping the leg of my jeans. I'd seen a lot of *Mannix* episodes on TVLand and couldn't recall a time Mannix ever ripped his pants pursuing a villain. They were new too. "Shit," I muttered as I scrambled back to my feet. I ran across the yard just as the lights in the house began to come on. Either the killer or I had roused the inhabitants. I could hear a small dog yapping inside.

I went around the corner of the house. There was no trace of the man in black. I stopped and tried to stretch out my senses but couldn't find a trace of him that way, either. Like I said, I'm not exactly psychic, more what I'd call finely attuned to the paranormal world. Nothing. I listened carefully, but all I could hear was the dog and someone shuffling about inside the house. I walked to the front of the house and down to the street. Looking both ways, I could see no sign of the man. I sighed and started back to the bar. My cell phone was in my car. I'd have to call 911 from there.

I took stock of my situation. I hadn't gotten very far figuring out where Brenda Sanderson was, and now I'd witnessed a murder. I didn't know if the two were connected, and I'd ripped my jeans. I found myself wishing I'd gone off to have sex with Craig. At least then I wouldn't be spending another night talking with the police.

CHAPTER 10

LIEUTENANT DAVE CARSON of the Indianapolis Police Department had known me for several years. It would be going too far to say that he liked me, but he didn't despise me either. I'd actually assisted him several times on cases, so he tolerated me. Naturally, I didn't tell him about Robbie the dead boyfriend, Daisy the Zombie Dog, or Gina the witch. I think doing so would have changed his opinion of me.

He was standing over the chalk outline of Bethany's body, looking down at it as if he expected to find a clue that everyone else had overlooked. The sun had come up and was bathing everything in that gray, unreal morning light. "So you didn't get a look at the guy's face." It wasn't a question.

"Nope."

"And you lost him at the end of the alley." Again, not a question.

"Yep."

Carson frowned at me. "What the hell are you involved in, Andrews?"

I'd actually been very honest with my answers, but I couldn't blame him for being suspicious. "This time I think I was just in the wrong place at the wrong time. I can't see how this had anything to do with Brenda Sanderson. Unless she's been murdered as well. Then you've got a serial killer on your hands."

"The thought had occurred to me." Carson didn't look happy.

"We've talked with your buddy, Craig…."

"He isn't my buddy. Just met him tonight."

Carson went on as if I hadn't interrupted. "And he pretty much confirms what you told us."

"The trust you have in me is underwhelming."

The tips of Carson's ears turned beet red. "Don't be a smart ass, Andrews. You're a good guy, at least when you keep out of my hair. If you find out anything that leads you to believe Sanderson is dead and we have a serial killer on our hands, I want you to let me know immediately."

I nodded. "Will do." I probably would, too, but I had a gut feeling that the killer wasn't anyone the police could handle. I recalled the strong sense of the otherworldly that the man in black had given off. I didn't think he was entirely human. Certainly not the sort of thing the IPD was used to dealing with.

Carson shook his head and examined the chalk outline again. "I've got a bad feeling about this one," he said.

I couldn't have agreed more.

SOMEONE *had seen him. The man was still boiling with anger. Some… nobody… had interrupted his sacrifice. He had been seen. He had been pursued.*

The man wasn't worried. He had been seen in the past when he'd been out getting the flesh. The authorities hadn't caught him then, and they wouldn't catch him now. No, the man was just annoyed that he hadn't been able to finish. He hadn't really been able to fully enjoy the kill.

The man put the key into the lock on his front door. He entered his house, not bothering to turn on any of the lights. He didn't need them. He took off his long black coat and tossed it onto a chair.

Rubbing a hand over his face, the man sighed. Next time he would make sure that he would have time. He would enjoy the hunt and the kill, and no one would interrupt him. There were plenty of girls in the city. He would find another.

It pleased the man to use wanton girls for the flesh. Girls who liked the way they looked. Girls who liked to show their bodies to men. They were the best. They reminded him of Angela. Angela, dead all those years ago, still haunted him.

Every time he plunged a knife into a girl, he thought of Angela. How she had laughed at him. He had killed her then, and he killed her still. Every woman he killed was Angela.

The man strode slowly into the kitchen. He was hungry. He needed to eat.

Liver sounded good right now.

CHAPTER 11

THE weather had taken a turn to the chilly side, so I wore a leather jacket when Gina and I took Daisy for a walk in Gustafson Park. It was dusk and technically the park, like all Indianapolis parks, closed at dusk, but I found that was the best time for Daisy. People tended to get upset when they saw a weird-looking bulldog chase and bite the head off a squirrel. Daisy was off her leash, another park no-no, so that she could build up the steam to catch her prey. Zombies, especially zombie dogs, don't move as slowly as they do in the movies. Otherwise, how would they ever get anything to eat? Wait around for that one idiot who twists his ankle running away from said zombie?

Gina, wearing a black cloak that went down almost to her ankles, watched as Daisy disappeared around a tree. We could hear the snap of bones as she caught up with dinner. "It's much easier to handle her feeding habits," she said, "when you don't actually have to see them."

"So true." I nodded at her cloak. "Don't people find it odd when you dress like a witch? I mean, shouldn't you go for the opposite look?"

She shook her head. "It's the 'Purloined Letter' approach. Dress like you are a witch and no one will suspect. Besides, people just think I'm Goth. Plus, very few people believe in witches anymore."

Daisy trotted back from the tree, licking squirrel blood from her muzzle. She smiled happily and ran a few circles around Gina and I before darting off again, presumably searching for dessert.

"You don't talk about your past much," I said. "I've known you for years, and while you know nearly everything about me, I don't know that much about you. There's not something really horrible that you've done, like the plague or anything like that, is there?"

She laughed. "What's up with you? Suddenly you want me to be on *This Is Your Life*? You've never voiced a concern about my past before."

"The murder of the stripper, Bethany, is bothering me. I'd swear the killer was paranormal in some way, but he wasn't a ghost. I wondered if he might be one of your kind."

"No way," Gina replied with a shake of her head. "Witches, at least true witches, are all but extinct. I'd know if there was another in Indianapolis. Closest one lives up in Mishawaka. I can say with certainty that your killer wasn't a witch."

"What was he, then?"

She shrugged. "No idea. You're the detective. You figure it out."

"He wasn't a zombie. No flesh was eaten."

"Maybe he didn't have time."

"Maybe," I said, not really believing it. "He was using a knife, though. A zombie wouldn't use a knife."

"True. They are very hands-on or, more accurately, teeth-on creatures."

Daisy was lost in the shadows among a small group of trees. I could just barely make out her form as she latched onto another squirrel. Once again we heard the crunch of bones. "Case in point," I said.

A light mist formed in the fading light and gathered near my left side, condensing and becoming human in form. In seconds Robbie coalesced and was walking beside us. "Find any good corpses lately?" he asked with a cheeky grin. He was wearing jeans and his high school letter jacket, presumably to hold off the chill night air that he couldn't feel. Old habits die hard, I guess.

"Just the usual number," I replied. Daisy, who could see Robbie even when I couldn't, came running up to him, her tongue out and lolling to one side. A fleck of bloody squirrel flesh hung off one of her teeth.

I saw Gina stiffen slightly when Robbie appeared. Ghosts were something that witches had no power over, so even though she and Robbie had never fallen out or argued, she never felt entirely comfortable in his presence. "Can't you," she asked him petulantly, "wear a cow bell or something so we can know when you're ready to appear? It's very disconcerting, you just popping up unannounced."

"I suppose I could always moan and rattle some chains about," Robbie said, "but only if you promise to travel by broom."

When I said they'd never argued, I didn't mean to imply that they didn't continually bicker.

I attached Daisy's leash to her collar and looked at Robbie. I never appreciated it when he wore his letter jacket, so I'm sure my face was a little sour, but these things can't be helped. Didn't he realize that it just accentuated his youthful appearance while I continued to age? "Any guesses as to what killed Bethany?"

Robbie gave it some thought. "It wasn't a ghost. No ghost I know of could kill someone with a knife like that. Hell, picking up a book and carrying it across a room wears me out. You're sure it was a knife? Could we be dealing with a werewolf?"

I realized that I hadn't actually seen the weapon, but I doubted Robbie was on to something. "The wounds didn't look like they'd been made by claws. Besides, I saw the guy. While I didn't exactly get a good look, I also didn't get the wolf vibe. He moved like a human."

"That's probably what he was," Gina said. "A human. Just a regular guy who likes to carve up young women. Nasty enough. Why does he have to be something more than that?"

"Because I got a strong psychic impression from him," I said. "Is there anything else otherworldly that he could be? Like a ghoul. What is a ghoul, anyway?"

Robbie and Gina exchanged a glance. "You don't want to know," Robbie said. "Let's just say she was moving when he attacked her, so it wasn't a ghoul."

I picked Daisy up and grabbed a rag from my back pocket. Best to be prepared and have something to wipe away blood and gore if you don't want it all over her muzzle for the rest of the night. Wiping away, I muttered, "Probably doesn't have anything to do with the case I'm working on anyway. Tomorrow I'm going to concentrate on finding Brenda Sanderson. I'll worry about the other if it becomes obvious the two are connected."

"They will be," Robbie foresaw. "With you, nothing is ever easy."

"Tell me about it."

CHAPTER 12

I MET with Craig and his sister Tiffany at a coffee shop on Massachusetts Avenue. It was close to noon and the place was packed. It took me forever to get a tall latte for Tiffany, an iced chai for Craig, and a Diet Pepsi for myself. When I brought the drinks back to our little table, I found out that my Diet was in fact a regular Pepsi. There was no way I was going to fight the line again, so I pushed it aside and tried not to let its presence taunt me. Craig and his sister sat across from me and they both looked a little pale, although I wasn't sure if that was from the events of the last few days or the fact that they weren't used to being up when the sun was shining.

"Isn't it awful, what happened to Bethany?" Tiffany was saying as I handed her drink to her. The excitement in her voice told me that while she may find it awful on some level, it was also quite a thrill. Tiffany was pretty in a sort of washed-out way. Too much drinking, too many late nights, and too much partying had robbed her of some of her spark. Had her life gone another way she could have been an actress or something similar. You could tell she'd been a stunner not that many years ago. As it was, a few more years and she'd look so worn that she'd have a hard time filling her G-string with dollar bills. I wondered what a stripper did when she retired.

"And to think it happened so close to where I was," Craig said, shaking his head. In the harsh light of day I was glad I hadn't gone home with him. The hair was still unwashed, but now I could see the blotchy skin and discolored fingernails. Had I really gotten to the point where someone like Craig would be acceptable? I steered the conversation away from the murder. My case was Brenda Sanderson. "What do you think has happened to Brenda?" I asked Tiffany. She looked blank for a moment so I threw the other name out to jar her memory. "Amber. Your friend who's disappeared."

Tiffany blew on her latte and took a tiny sip. "You mean do I think she was murdered too?"

"It's a possibility."

She shook her head. "No, Amber wasn't the sort to get herself murdered. She ran off with her guy. I'd bet you anything on that."

I wondered what it was that made Bethany the sort that would get herself murdered but forgot about that at the mention of a guy. "She was seeing someone?"

"A guy named Derek Schneider." Tiffany made a face. I couldn't tell if she didn't like Derek or her latte or both. "He started coming to the club a couple of months ago. Really surprised me when they started going out. He was kind of a low-life. Not really her type at all."

He might not have been her type, but he probably was just the type that Janice Sanderson would have a heart attack over her daughter seeing. "Know where this guy lived?"

Tiffany thought it over. She either really wasn't used to being up at this hour or thinking for her required a lot of work. "Somewhere on the south side. I remember she said something about going to his place one time. Apparently he lives with his sister and her family, or something like that. Amber was pretty disgusted, I could tell. Kids running all over the place, the place a wreck. She said there must have been six kids and three adults living in a tiny little three bedroom house. She said it smelled, and they couldn't make out because there was nowhere to do it. I laughed when she told me, but you could tell Amber didn't see the humor in it."

"Know where this Derek worked?"

"A junkyard, I think. Or some sort of used car lot. I remember him talking about car parts one night. No, it was a junkyard. Run by his uncle, I believe. Yeah, I remember now. His uncle paid him under the counter when he needed work. The rest of the time I think Derek just sold pot to the local school kids. He never had much money, that's for sure."

"Yet he could afford to hang out at Pickin's."

She shrugged. "You do what you gotta do. I think after they started seeing each other that Amber paid his cover to get in. He didn't drink much, and I never saw him tip any of the girls, except Amber. And even then not much."

Quite the Romeo. "Anyone else show interest in Amber other than this Derek? Any guy that seemed to come just to watch her dance?"

Tiffany shook her head. "Not that I remember."

During this conversation Craig had kept his eyes on me. He exuded boredom and had almost finished his chai. When his sister seemed to run out of words she knew to say he spoke up. "Do you think the girls at Pickin's are in danger from some sort of maniac killer? Is Tiff in any danger?"

"It's hard to say. Bethany's death may have been an isolated incident, but I certainly wouldn't take any chances." I gave Tiffany a stern look. "I wouldn't go home with any strangers, or go outside at night unless you're with someone."

"You think Amber is dead, and they just haven't found the body yet?" Craig asked.

"It's possible. I hope not."

"You saw Bethany's body, right?" Craig asked.

"Yep."

"What did she look like?"

"Dead," I said. "She looked very, very dead."

IT WAS in their eyes. Angela had that look. The one that said I'm better than you.

He never should have become involved with Angela. His kind never mixed with humans. Not while they were alive, anyway. Angela had lived next door to his cemetery. At that time, he had been staying in a crypt just outside of London. It was a nice area. Lots of trees and even a stream not far away. Angela and her mother lived in the old rectory. He didn't know it when he first met her, but Angela had been hauled out to the countryside forcibly by her mother. Angela's mother assumed that if she took her daughter away from the sins of the city, Angela would somehow change. She shouldn't have bothered.

Angela had been in the garden the first time the man saw her. He hadn't been a man then, of course. But he now thought of himself as human (mostly) and refused to think of himself as anything else. Angela had stolen out into the night. She had climbed out of an upstairs window and down a tree. The man had been scavenging and had happened to glance at the house as Angela had made her escape. He had never seen anyone so... enchanting. The way she moved. The way she looked. He wanted her. Not like he wanted other humans. No, he wanted to... protect her. The concept had been foreign to him, but he knew that's what he wanted. He wanted to make sure that she came to no harm.

He followed at a discreet distance as Angela walked down the road in the moonlight. She was heading for the town. He knew she was going to the inn. It was the only place in town to go at night.

He was right. Angela walked swiftly, with purpose, and made her way to the Lion's Mane. She stayed there for several hours. The man waited outside. He couldn't go in, of course, but he wanted to be sure Angela would come to no harm.

When she left and walked back down the road, swaying slightly, the man followed again. He listened as she hummed a tune. The notes seemed so sweet in the night air, and it felt like she was singing only to him.

CHAPTER 13

THE Boyd house certainly wasn't what you'd think of as a haunted house. It was a typical suburban ranch house, with white aluminum siding and hunter green window shutters. There was a pink girl's bicycle on the front porch. Ellen Boyd answered my knock. She looked like she hadn't slept much since I'd seen her. Before she let me in, she gave me a warning. "Tanner's furious that I've talked to you about this. He says you're just going to take my money for nothing."

"And what do you think?"

She closed her eyes wearily. "I want this done."

The inside of the house was tastefully furnished and was a bit of a surprise. Ellen Boyd had either had an interior designer in or had a knack for decorating. The front door led into the living room, and it could have come straight from a magazine. Even with the bright cheeriness of the room, though, I could feel that something was amiss as soon as I stepped inside. "Nice place," I said, more to try to relax Ellen than anything else. I examined my reflection in the large mirror over the fireplace. I was also looking for any anomalies in the glass. Spirits like hiding in mirrors.

She smiled slightly. "I like to make things nice for my family."

A man entered from the hall, obviously having heard our voices. Tanner Boyd was tall and muscular and looked more like a college football player than a married father of two. If I hadn't known better, I'd have guessed his age in the mid-twenties, maximum. He was wearing jeans and an Indianapolis Colts jersey. With his long brown hair and his well-developed biceps, Tanner Boyd didn't seem to fit either the house or his wife. He shot me an angry glare.

"You must be the detective, Duncan Andrews."

"I must be." I didn't offer to shake hands with him. His Machoness would only try to squeeze the hell out of my fingers.

He stepped up to me and looked down his nose to get a good look at me. He was several inches taller than me, and I'm sure he thought I'd be intimidated. I wasn't. I know how to kick someone in the balls if I have to.

"You don't look like a detective," he said.

"I know," I replied. "I'm much too pretty."

Ellen Boyd stepped between us and glared at her husband. "Tanner, Mr. Andrews is here as my guest, and I expect him to be treated as such."

Tanner tried to look innocent. "What? I just said he didn't look like a detective."

"You know what I mean," she said. Turning to me, she asked, "Would you like to see the rest of the house, Mr. Andrews?"

Before I could answer Tanner butted in, shaking his head. "I still say there's nothing here for him to look into. Just a lot of overactive imaginations."

I shrugged. "If that's the case, then this won't take very long, and I'll be out of your hair before you know it."

Boyd didn't look happy, but his wife took me by the elbow and showed me around the house. There was a sizable kitchen which kept the color scheme of white and hunter green going, three bedrooms, two bathrooms, and a den. The living room seemed to be the hub for most of the home's activity, and it was there that I had the strongest feeling of something paranormal in the air. When we returned it was even stronger. Ellen Boyd was jumpy and kept looking over her shoulder as if expecting to find a specter in every darkened corner.

Tanner Boyd, despite his insistence that we were wasting our time and that the existence of ghosts was but a foolish notion, was just as wary. He walked on the balls of his feet, ready for action. I'm not sure what action he was expecting to take. It might have been flight or punching me in the face. I was hoping for flight.

Outside the sun was fading and some rather nasty storm clouds had appeared, making the night come on a little quicker than normal for the time of year. Ellen turned on several lamps around the living room, her hand shaking a little. She crossed her arms and rubbed her biceps briskly. "It's cold in here," she said, a note of apology in her voice.

"Actually, it isn't," I said. I walked over to her and waved my hand in the air in front of her. "Something is drawing in energy, trying to manifest. That's what's causing the cold spot."

Tanner snorted. "That's ridiculous. It's just a draft coming from a vent or something. Really, the sooner we get this ghost nonsense out of everyone's heads—"

He stopped because the logs in the fireplace suddenly ignited. I could feel a wave of heat as it crossed the room. The lamps that Ellen had lit suddenly went out and the room was lit solely by the blaze that had spontaneously started. Tanner, who was closest to the fireplace, paled as he stared in disbelief at the flames.

"A spark, that's what it was. Some spark that just hit the right bit of wood...."

"Yeah," I said, "that's a convincing argument. Now try explaining why some of the smoke is blue."

Among the orange and yellow tendrils of flame leaping up was a thin stream of blue smoke. The stream rose and got thicker. The blue smoke came forward out of the fireplace and began to form a figure. Ellen Boyd gave a strangled yelp as she covered her mouth with both hands. Tanner rocked back and forth, his eyes registering shock.

In moments a female figure stood in front of the fireplace. She looked to be in her late twenties and was obviously the same spirit that had been spotted previously by Ellen Boyd. Unlike Robbie, this spirit seemed unable to appear in any color other than blue, so details such as hair or eye color were impossible. The ghost slowly turned her head, taking in the three of us. She then turned to Tanner and raised her hand, pointing a finger at him. Her mouth opened and an unholy wail filled the room.

Tanner chose flight. Unfortunately he didn't plan his escape route well, and his shins collided hard with the coffee table. He fell but quickly scrambled back to his feet and was out of the room in seconds. I heard a back door opening and slamming shut.

As soon as Tanner was gone the ghost vanished. The flames slowly died in the fireplace and finally extinguished with a small hiss. Once the last lick of flame was gone, the lights came back up. I looked at Ellen Boyd.

"I'd say that you were right. Not only do you have a ghost, but the ghost and your husband seem to have a connection."

Ellen, her hands still covering her mouth, merely nodded.

CHAPTER 14

IT WASN'T difficult to find the junkyard where, according to Tiffany, Bethany's boyfriend Derek worked. Just off of Tibbs in one of the seedier sections of the south side, I found Schneider's Junk Yard. The place was surrounded by a huge wooden fence with a gate in front that was kept open during business hours. Schneider's Junk Yard was painted on the gate in red letters. I pulled in and found a place to park. There was a small office that looked like a good wind would knock it over. Everywhere else there was just trash and rubbish and a lot of cars in various stages of dilapidation. Derek's uncle seemed to make most of his money from selling parts off of junked cars. In front of the office were sundry other items that Schneider's had that one could pick up for a song. An out-of-tune song, at that. A swing set that was nearly eaten away with rust. Three baby strollers, one with a broken wheel. An Easy Bake Oven that looked like it had been dragged through the mud. I wouldn't give the change in my pocket for the lot.

Grass refused to grow within the fenced-in area, and I can't say I blamed it. I kicked up a little dust as I walked up to the office door. There was a small, broken wooden step in front of the door that showed traces of rat droppings. I'd have to remember to bring Daisy here next time so she could feed. A sign said to Come On In, so I did.

Inside everything looked to be coated with oil or dust or both, including the guy sitting behind the counter. He was watching a tiny black and white television and barely looked up when I entered. Oprah is hard to tear yourself away from.

"You're Schneider?" I asked.

He waited until the commercial and then leaned forward to turn the sound down. "Who wants to know?" Schneider was a big guy, but not a healthy big. His grimy shirt didn't entirely cover his gut, and I was subjected to the sight of his fish-belly-white stomach. He had sandals on over white socks. Classy guy.

"Me. My name is Duncan Andrews. I'm looking for your nephew, Derek."

Schneider barked out a harsh laugh. "He owe you money? Good luck with that, partner. You'll never see any of it. Boy was supposed to come and help out here today and never did show up. Just works when he feels like it, I guess." For someone who didn't want to talk to me at first, he'd suddenly become quite garrulous. Must be my winning personality.

"He doesn't owe me money. Just need to see him, that's all."

Schneider cocked an eyebrow at me, and I could see understanding dawn upon him. He obviously thought I wanted to buy some weed off his nephew. He nodded. "He's living down on Gimber right now, few blocks over." He gave me the address. "He's probably there right now, sitting on his ass. Boy'll do anything to keep from working."

I thanked him and beat a hasty retreat. I felt like I needed a shower, and I hadn't even touched anything in the office. I got back in my car and drove around until I found Gimber Street. As I searched house numbers, I thought about calling Ellen Boyd to check in with her but nixed the idea. She knew how to get in touch with me if there were any fresh developments. After running out of the house, Tanner Boyd had apparently made a beeline for his favorite bar. Upon returning, he still insisted that ghosts don't exist and that what we'd seen was some sort of shared illusion. Apparently this was the same illusion that allowed people to believe that Liberace was straight.

The house where Derek Schneider was living was indeed small. I found a parking spot on the street a few houses down and walked back. Several kids were playing in the front yard. They all wore dirty clothes and none had on a jacket despite the chill in the air. The oldest was a boy of about seven or eight. He was digging into the dirt with a pocket knife. A sullen-looking girl of about five was standing by watching him. Two other boys were wrestling off to the side. They seemed to be getting a bit angry and were cussing each other out with words I wouldn't think six year olds knew. The other kids paid them no attention.

The kid with the knife looked up as I approached. Not finding me of interest, he went back to his digging. I went on up to the front door and knocked. After a moment the door was opened by a boy wearing cut-off jeans with the top of his boxer shorts in plain view. A fashion guru. He had blond hair and was maybe fourteen. He looked at me like I was a slug. "Yeah?" he asked.

"I'm looking for Derek," I said with a friendly smile.

He was immune to my charm. "Ain't here," he said.

"Do you know where he is?"

The kid gave an almost imperceptible shake of his head. He didn't know, and he didn't care. I couldn't see much of the inside of the house, as the kid hadn't opened the door more than was necessary, but I could see that the small living room behind him had a pair of bunk beds pressed up against one wall. A television was on and some unseen person or persons were in the middle of a video game. I guessed I was keeping Blondie from blowing up a planet or whatever the object of the game was. "How about Amber?" I asked. "Is she around?"

He looked at me blankly.

"Brenda?"

The same look. I wanted to punch the kid. I couldn't tell if the name meant nothing to him or if he'd merely decided I wasn't worth giving any information. "Check back later," he said, starting to swing the door closed. "Derek should be back then."

I let the door close. Despite the lack of verbal confirmation, I was pretty sure I'd found where Brenda Sanderson had gone. Derek must be one hell of a lay or, more likely, she really wanted to get back at her mother to endure staying at this kid-infested hovel.

Back in the yard, the two boys had found that wrestling wasn't settling their differences and one was straddling the other and throwing punches. Most were deflected by the other boy's upraised arms, but it was still quite a beating. The kid on the bottom was screaming at the top of his lungs. The boy with the knife didn't even bother looking up. "Stop it, you two," he threatened, "or I'll come over there and stop you myself."

They ignored him. I smiled at the little girl as I walked by. Her mouth shifted slightly, which I took as an attempt at a smile. I got back into my car and wished that I didn't have to return. Maybe I could just provide Janice Sanderson with the address and tell her that's where her daughter was. Let her deal with the Brady Bunch from Hell.

I sighed and started the engine. I needed a drink. I'd have to drive through downtown to get back home, so I figured I'd stop off at Jimmy's, a gay bar on Pennsylvania Avenue. It was a piano bar and a popular place for the after-work crowd. I'd found the place where Brenda Sanderson *may* have run to, so I considered that I'd done some work and therefore qualified to join the after-work crowd.

As I pulled away I looked in my rear view mirror and saw that the two boys had risen. The one that had been getting the snot beat out of him picked up a toy tractor and threw it at the other kid. It hit the kid in the forehead, and I could hear his howl even with the engine running and the windows all up.

I pressed the accelerator and gunned down the street. A gin and tonic or two would make the day seem a little better.

ANGELA had taken to sneaking out of her house often to spend time down at the Lion's Mane. The young men in town began to talk about her. The things they said angered the man. Once he was at the edge of the cemetery and happened to overhear a conversation between two men on the other side of the fence. They were taking a shortcut through the churchyard on their way home. Usually the man paid no attention to people when they talked, but he overheard one of them mention Angela. By now the man knew her name. He often heard Angela's mother calling out for her, usually in anger. The man was laughing and calling Angela a whore.

He followed the two men. He stayed back, making sure they didn't know they were being followed. He was getting very good at being stealthy. Angela never suspected that she was being followed to the inn night after night. The taller of the two men, a youth with a broken nose and bad skin, continued to laugh and speak ill of Angela. When the two men separated, he followed the tall man.

He killed the youth with the broken nose, strangled him with his hands. Then he clawed his way into the youth's gut and ate some liver. It tasted good. Fresh. It was the first time the man had killed and the first time he had tasted new flesh. It was so different from already-dead flesh. He liked it.

He also knew that he was changing in some way. He was no longer one of his own kind. Not exactly. He wasn't human, either, but he no longer wanted to skulk and hide in the shadows. He wanted to be free of the cemetery. He wanted to be with Angela.

He took the young man's heart with him and ate it back at the crypt.

CHAPTER 15

ONCE I turned onto Pennsylvania Avenue, Robbie appeared in the passenger seat next to me. As always during daylight hours he seemed somewhat faded, as if I was seeing him through a veil of gauze. He was wearing jeans and a tight T-shirt which showed off his wrestler's build. He slumped in the seat so that his knees connected with the dashboard, the picture of sullenness. "Where you going?" he asked, trying and failing to sound nonchalant about it.

"Jimmy's Bar for a drink or two," I said, "and then some food before I head back to the south side and hopefully wrap this case up."

He turned to gaze out the window, still feigning indifference. "Jimmy's," he said.

"Yes."

"A gay bar."

"Yes."

He let a few beats go by. "You can get alcohol anywhere. You don't have to go to a gay bar."

"I feel more comfortable in a gay bar," I said.

Robbie still refused to look my way. "Wouldn't be any other reason for going there, would there?"

"Such as?" I asked as I pulled into the lot next to Jimmy's.

Robbie sighed heavily. "You're looking to meet someone new, aren't you?"

I found a spot and pulled in. Shutting off the engine, I turned to Robbie, who was studying an imaginary fleck of dust on the knee of his jeans. "I'm not actively going out to find someone to date, if that's what you're thinking," I said. "But if it happens, it happens."

He picked at an imaginary piece of lint. "So it's over between us," he said in a low voice.

"Robbie," I said gently, "technically speaking, it's been over for us for ten years now. You're dead."

"I know!" He planted his feet on the floor with a stomp, which indicated just how upset he was. To make any sound (including speaking) costs him spectral energy. To create a bang like that took a lot out of him. As I watched he faded even more.

"I'll always love you, Robbie," I said. "You know that. But at the risk of sounding like an article in *Cosmopolitan,* I have… needs."

He snorted at that. "You've got your hand," he said.

"It's not the same thing, and you know it. You may not look like you're aging, but I am. I don't want to wait until I'm old to have someone else hold me."

Robbie reluctantly nodded. "My feelings for you haven't changed, though."

"Nor have mine for you," I assured him. "You've got to admit, though, our situation is a little odd. With most people, death kind of puts an end to the relationship. They generally don't go on seeing each other on a regular basis."

"True," he conceded.

We sat in silence for several minutes. If anyone had walked by, they would have thought I was sitting alone in my car, staring off into space. No one did. Eventually I said, "I'll take things slowly. I won't just jump into something, and I promise I'll keep your feelings in mind at all times."

He shifted in his seat as if trying to find a comfortable position. I knew he was just pausing to come up with the right words. When it became obvious that I wasn't going to bail him out and break the silence, he spoke. "I know this can't be easy for you. I just... I just don't want you to forget me."

Hardly likely, with him haunting me on a daily basis. I knew what he meant, though. "I never could," I said.

Robbie nodded and faded from sight. I thought I saw a tear roll down his cheek just as he vanished completely.

JIMMY'S wasn't exactly packed, but it wasn't a bad crowd, either, for Happy Hour. There was no one at the piano in the corner nor was there any music playing over the loudspeakers, so conversations could actually be conducted without shouting. I found a spot near the middle of the bar and sat down. The stools on either side of me were vacant. I figured that way Robbie couldn't accuse me of trying to sidle up next to some cutie, not that he could see me.

I ordered a gin and tonic, and as I drank it, I took stock. It seemed like my missing-persons case was nearly over. If indeed Brenda Sanderson was living with Derek Schneider in the House of Too Many Kids then she, and therefore I, had nothing to do with the mysterious killer of Bethany the stripper. Well, nothing other than I was a witness. Robbie, while not overly fond of the idea, at least seemed resigned to the notion of me beginning to date. Things were looking up. I decided on a second gin and tonic. Just as the bartender was setting it down in front of me someone sat down on the stool to my right. I told myself not to look. Once you do that, of course, you have to look. I resisted the temptation but finally gave in.

He was maybe thirty, a few years younger than me. He had short black hair and a roundish face. It was a nice face. He wasn't dressed in a suit like most of Jimmy's patrons who'd come from downtown office buildings. Like me he wore jeans and a collared knit shirt. He probably sat next to me because I was the only other person in the place that didn't look like a lawyer or an accountant. He smiled at me.

I smiled back and then felt embarrassed, so I looked at my drink. I so wasn't used to flirting.

Not deterred by my lack of continued eye contact, he said, "Nice day."

Not an auspicious start. I didn't do much better with my reply. "Yes, it is."

His smile broadened. "I'm Nick." He stuck out his hand. I shook it.

"Duncan."

Admittedly, I was horribly out of practice, but I was astonished at how hard it was to hold a conversation with a stranger with the idea of seeing how well-matched romantically you could be. I searched for a question to ask but couldn't think of one that wasn't immensely stupid. He took a long pull from his beer and asked a question of his own.

"So what do you do?"

"I'm a private detective."

"Really?" He seemed suitably impressed. "I didn't think they existed outside of mystery stories."

"There are a few of us in the world. Most work for big companies. I'm just a one-man operation." Okay, one man, a ghost, a zombie dog, and a witch if you want to be technical and list helpers, but he didn't need to know that. The knowledge would only make him change seats to get far away from me. "What do you do?" I asked.

"I'm a teacher. I teach history at Paul Davis High School. I also am the assistant coach for the basketball and wrestling teams."

Robbie had gone to Paul Davis and been on the wrestling team. Ten years ago would probably have been before Nick's time, but I didn't want to take a chance and ask if he remembered him. Why was I thinking of Robbie anyway? Nick. Think of Nick.

"It must be exciting, being a detective," he said.

"Usually not. Rarely do I get a chance to look for Maltese Falcons."

Nick glanced at his watch and shook his head. "Hey, I hate to be forward, but I have to be somewhere in a few minutes."

"That's not being forward."

"Well," he said with a shy smile, "I was going to ask you for your phone number so I could ask you to dinner or something. I'd hate to lose a chance of going out with a hot guy like you just because I'm short of time."

"I'd hate for that to happen as well," I said. I had a few of my business cards in my wallet, but that seemed a little ostentatious, so I got a matchbook and pen from the bartender. At the last second I nearly changed one of the numbers so that he couldn't contact me. *Don't be a chicken,* I told myself as I jotted down the last number. *He wants to ask you on a date, not to move in with him.*

"Cool," he said, pocketing the number. "I'll give you a call."

I wasn't sure if I wanted him to or not. Was I ready to date? Okay, it had been a long time, but I still had my old boyfriend literally hanging around. Yes, I was ready. Yes, I wanted him to call. No, I didn't. Yeah. No.

Another gin and tonic was in order.

THE man—and surely he was more man than creature now—continued to watch over Angela. For her, he began to mimic other men. He stole some clothes and even started bathing in the stream that flowed not far from his crypt. He thought of a name for himself, since men had names. Now he was Caleb, a name he'd heard at one of the many funeral services held at his cemetery. He fancied that the name was appropriate, since he'd been the one who killed the young man they were burying. Caleb had beaten the young man to death. The young man had been armed with a knife, not that it had done him much good. Caleb took the knife and used it to cut out the man's liver.

Much better than clawing one's way into the body. Liver. Fresh flesh. Just as good the next day, too, as Caleb had brought bits back to his crypt. Much better than the long-dead flesh he was used to eating.

Angela didn't know he existed, but that would soon change. He was becoming more and more human. And he knew of a way to become even more of a man. There had been stories among his people of a magic talisman. An amulet of great power, the talisman was said to be buried in Wales. Luckily things buried in graveyards were often known by his kind. Caleb had always enjoyed stories, and he knew everything his people could tell him about the amulet. He was certain he could find it. Normally travel was difficult for his kind, as they had to avoid contact with humans. That was no longer a problem for Caleb. He was a man now. And when he became fully human, he'd go to Angela and tell her of his love ....

CHAPTER 16

FORTIFIED with food and more gin than was probably good for me, I headed back down to the south side. I had stopped off at my apartment to pick up Daisy with the intention of getting her some food after chatting with Brenda Sanderson. Hey, a zombie dog has gotta eat.

As I was loading Daisy into the car my cell phone rang. It was Ellen Boyd.

"Is anything wrong?" I asked, noting the fear in her voice.

"I'm not sure," she answered.

"Have you seen the spirit again?"

"No, it's not that," Ellen replied slowly. "It's Tanner. He's been acting peculiar."

More peculiar than when I'd met him? "How do you mean?"

"It's hard to put my finger on it. He just has these moments when it's like he's not even here. Like he's listening to something in his head."

Daisy, on the passenger seat, gave me a plaintive bark to let me know she was ready to roll. "Do you feel you're in any immediate danger?" I asked. I wanted to get down to Gimber Street to finish up the Sanderson case so I could concentrate all of my efforts on Ellen's problems.

"No," she replied. "He's at work right now and won't be home until late."

"I'm finishing up a case right now," I told her. "Would it be okay if I stopped by first thing in the morning?"

She said that would be fine, so I rang off and started down the road, Daisy growling softly in anticipation of adventure by my side.

BY THE time I pulled up in front of the house on Gimber, it was getting dark. No kids were digging or fighting in the yard. I could, however, hear yelling from inside the house. Home sweet home.

A short, rather rotund woman with a haggard face answered my knock. She didn't look like she'd been happy for years. With that many people living in a small house, who could blame her?

She looked at me and then past me to my car. I'd left the passenger window mostly open so that Daisy could get some air. She didn't need it, being dead, but she seemed to still expect it. Besides, leave even a zombie dog in a car with all the windows rolled up and some animal activist is sure to walk by and give you hell. In the fading light Daisy's eyes almost glowed red. I could see the surprise in the woman's face.

"Who are you?" she asked. She only gave me the briefest of glances before returning her attention to the car and Daisy. Really, it was as if she'd never seen a zombie dog before. Some people.

"I'm looking for Derek," I said.

"Derek!" She had to yell loud to be heard over the din in the house.

From inside someone shouted back, "What?"

"Someone here wants to see you!" Before Derek even came to the door she vacated her watch, giving one last shuddery glance at Daisy. Maybe she went to quiet some of the kids. If so, she failed. The door remained open so I peeked inside. In the living room several kids were seated right in front of the television set watching cartoons. With all the hollering going on, I wondered how anyone could hear what SpongeBob was saying. I also wondered if the kids ever slept, as it was getting late and tomorrow would be a school day for them.

After a few minutes, a young man appeared. He wore torn jeans and an unbuttoned baseball shirt. His blond hair was trimmed so short that at first I thought he was bald. "Yes," he asked, glaring at me.

"Derek Schneider?" I asked.

He looked me over and apparently came to the conclusion that I wasn't a threat. He was pretty muscular and had a good ten pounds on me, so he was undoubtedly right. He nodded.

"My name is Duncan Andrews. I'm actually looking for Brenda Sanderson. I have reason to believe she might be staying here."

He immediately tensed up, squaring his shoulders. "What makes you say that?"

"Well, you, for one thing," I said. "If she wasn't here, you'd have said who wants to know or given me a flat out denial that she was here. As it is—"

I didn't see the punch coming. That's what I get for enjoying the sound of my own voice. Derek slammed his right fist into my gut, doubling me over. As I bent he hit me again, this time with a nice left hook. If my body wasn't screaming from the jolt of pain, I might have admired his technique. As it was, I fell back, landing on my keister in the dirt. I was shaking the cobwebs out of my brain and trying to scramble back to my feet when I saw a small blur go by me. It wasn't until I heard an agonized yell from Derek that I realized that Daisy had bolted from the car and was even now attacking Derek. When the mental fog lifted, and I could actually see clearly, I saw Derek hopping on the rickety steps, trying to dislodge the dog that had clamped onto his calf. With a tearing of cloth Daisy managed to bite a large chunk of his flesh. She gobbled it happily.

I got to my feet, holding my aching jaw. Derek had both hands covering his wound and was cursing up a storm. Blood was gushing all over his hands. He hadn't had all that much color to begin with.

Now his pallor resembled that of Robbie on a sunny day.

"That dog bit me!" Pain made his voice come out as a squeak. "I think it wants to eat me!"

Indeed, Daisy was watching him carefully and licking her chops, wondering if another taste of Derek might be in order.

A smallish young woman with extremely large breasts came bounding out of the house. She threw her arms around Derek and shouted, "Oh, baby, are you hurt?"

I'd found Brenda Sanderson.

CHAPTER 17

WE WERE in my car, speeding across town to Gina's house. It had taken a lot of cajoling, pleading, and demanding before I finally got Brenda and Derek to get in the car. They thought I was taking Derek to a hospital, and I let them go on thinking that. I had ripped a long strip off the bottom of my shirt to tie around Derek's leg, which seemed to help, although I had no idea what extra damage, if any, would result from a bite from a zombie. I was fairly sure that Derek wouldn't become a zombie himself. Fairly sure.

Derek sat up in the front with me, cursing under his breath and holding his leg. Brenda was in the back, holding Daisy on her lap. Getting her to go anywhere near the dog had been a monumental effort, but once this was accomplished, Brenda seemed to take to Daisy and vice versa.

"I don't think this dog is breathing," she said.

"She doesn't much," I admitted. "It's a long story."

"She sure can bite," Derek moaned. He looked at me, suddenly looking like a little kid despite his size. "Sorry about hitting you, dude. I thought you were a cop or someone Mrs. Sanderson sent out to get Brenda. I figured she found out we got married."

"I am someone Mrs. Sanderson sent out to get Brenda," I told him. "And a cop? You'd hit a cop like that?"

"Hey! I wasn't thinking, okay?" He still wasn't sure he liked me, but I was taking him to get his leg fixed up, so he at least trusted me for the moment.

"Seriously," said Brenda, "I don't think this dog is breathing at all."

"Her respiration is so slow that it's barely noticeable, but she's fine," I said. I frowned. "Did you say you two were married?"

"She's looking at me, and her eyes are moving, but I swear there's something wrong with her. When her eyes catch the light, they sort of glow. It's really creepy." In the rear view mirror I could see Brenda holding Daisy close to her. "And yeah, we got married."

I sighed. "That's Daisy. She's a zombie. You're safe, though, as long as you don't try to harm me."

"You mean like *Dawn of the Dead* zombie?" Brenda asked.

"Sort of."

I looked again in the rear view so I could see her face. She looked skeptical but not entirely unbelieving. Derek was too busy clutching at his leg and muttering expletives every few seconds to pay attention to what I'd said.

I pulled into Gina's neighborhood, a well-to-do area with a plethora of Tudor style houses. I heard Brenda shift nervously in her seat. "I don't think there's a hospital near here," she said.

"I said I'd take you to someone who could help his leg. I didn't say anything about a hospital."

Derek grew silent. I glanced over and saw that he was still conscious, but that was about it. I sped up and raced the rest of the way down the end of the street to where Gina's cottage stood.

Like its neighbors, Gina's house was in the Tudor style but on a much smaller scale. A wooden sign on her front lawn announced that here one could get a Tarot reading from Madame Gina. No prices were listed, but I knew she was on the pricey side. On the other hand, they were *true* readings. If Gina told you that you were going to marry a tall man from Boise, Idaho, you'd better start looking for a dress.

As I pulled into the drive, Derek leaned over, unable to hold himself upright any longer. He knocked against me making a sound somewhat like gas escaping from a pipe just as I came to a stop.

"Help me with him," I said to Brenda as I got out of the car. She set Daisy down onto the seat and got out herself. Daisy yapped as I went around and started to pull Derek out of the car. She still wasn't sure if he was a threat or not, but she knew he tasted good. Daisy licked her lips and snorted. Derek weighed more than me and was pretty much dead weight, so it was quite a struggle getting him to his feet. Brenda Sanderson was no help at all. She just stood by making hand gestures and suggesting that I get his arm around my shoulders, which, strangely, had already occurred to me. The jostling had revived Derek enough so he was able to assist me a little. At least we stayed upright all the way to Gina's door, although progress was slow. Brenda followed behind us, giving me helpful suggestions, most of which involved not dropping her boyfriend.

Gina answered the door in her usual voluminous blouse, earrings dangling nearly to her shoulders. I'd called her on my cell along the way, so she had been expecting us.

"Bring him into the living room," she instructed, "and get him onto the sofa."

Her living room was somewhat dim as she preferred candlelight to anything else. It seemed like there were hundreds of them lit, spread across the fireplace mantle, the coffee table, and any other surface that would hold one.

Derek groaned loudly as I set him as gently as possible onto the couch.

"He's still alive, at any rate," Gina said.

"It was just a dog bite, wasn't it?" a worried Brenda asked.

"Daisy," Gina said, icicles dripping from her voice, "is no ordinary dog. Her bite can be very, very dangerous." I thought Gina was laying it on a bit thick, but then I knew she had little patience with humans, especially those with no affinity for the paranormal. I felt sorry for the dentist she was dating.

Gina took a pair of scissors off the coffee table and cut away the bottom part of Derek's pant leg, revealing the still-seeping wound. I had to admit it looked quite nasty. The skin around the bite was turning white and seemed to be blistering. "There is a venom in the bite of a zombie," Gina explained to Brenda. "If the victim dies, it is this venom that causes the person to become a zombie himself. Daisy instinctively bites the heads off of her prey, otherwise there would be a small army of zombie squirrels and rats in Indianapolis by now."

It may have been the sight of Derek's wound or the talk of zombies, but Brenda seemed to have switched herself off. She was looking at Derek, but her eyes were devoid of intelligence.

"Take her into the den and get her some brandy," Gina said. "I'll take care of things in here."

Gina's den was a small room lined with bookcases and filled with comfortable chairs, each with its own reading lamp. The books were mainly spell books and long forgotten tomes, although there was one shelf filled, incongruously but tellingly, with hardcover editions of Danielle Steele novels.

I steered Brenda over to one of the chairs and deposited her. I found a brandy decanter on the sideboard and poured a generous snifter. Brenda sipped at it and coughed, but at least she'd rejoined the living.

"Don't worry about a thing," I told her. "Gina will take care of him. She's got a healing spell that works wonders."

"Spell?" Brenda blinked. "You talk about her like she's some kind of a witch."

"Yep," I said.

GINA was over an hour muttering incantations over Derek and smothering the wound with ointments. When Brenda and I returned to the living room, we found Derek sitting up and looking much better.

He was still pale, but he was smiling weakly. A large gauze bandage covered his calf.

"How are you feeling?" I asked him.

"Tons better," he replied. "She's a miracle worker. "

Gina was beaming, obviously pleased with herself. "Not bad, if I do say so myself."

Brenda, however, was eying the bandaged leg warily. "I thought it would be totally healed, like it had never happened. I mean, she's a witch, right? What sort of magic is there to putting a bandage on it?"

Gina's brow furrowed. "I'm a witch, not fucking Harry Potter. You want miracles, call the *700 Club*. I've removed the poison and treated the wound. After a week or two all he'll have to remember this by will be a scar. What more do you want?"

Pissing off a witch who has lived for several centuries isn't a smart thing to do. "You've done great," I assured Gina, quickly gathering Brenda and Derek and herding them toward the door. "We'll get out of your hair now. I'll give you a call tomorrow."

There was silence in the car for most of the trip back to the south side. Daisy sat in the front with me while Brenda cuddled against Derek in the back. When we got within a few blocks of Gimber Street, Brenda finally spoke up. "My mom paid you to come and find me."

"Yep."

"And you're going to tell her where I am?"

I nodded. "You had seemingly fallen off the face of the earth. She just wanted to know where you were, and that you were safe. Nothing says you have to go back and live with her, though or even see her. You're an adult. Hell, you're a married woman. You might let Tiffany and the people at work know that you're all right, though. They're worried about you."

"I don't want to talk to any of them," Brenda said glumly. "They'll all just say that Derek is no good and isn't right for me. Even

Tiffany says that. Like she's got room to talk!"

I found a parking spot near Derek's house and pulled in. Leaving the engine running, I turned to look at the couple clutching each other in the back. "Let me give you some unwanted advice," I said. "You're old enough to live your life any way you choose, regardless of what your mother or your roommate thinks. Bring Derek around to meet your mother. If she doesn't like him, that's her problem. At least you've tried. But don't run away from your friends and your family just because they don't like your taste in men."

She nodded listlessly as she and Derek got out of the car. I couldn't tell if she was going to take my advice, and I couldn't care less. My jaw still ached, and I wanted to go home and get some sleep.

Derek said goodbye and as the door closed shut, he once again apologized for punching me. I told him not to worry about it. I was through with the Sandersons, or so I thought.

The next morning I learned that while Gina was doing her healing routine, another stripper was murdered not more than ten blocks from her house.

CHAPTER 18

CONNIE BALLARD, or Skye if one chooses to use her dancing name, was found behind a Dumpster just off of East Street at six a.m. on September 4 by a guy walking his dog. This time the killer hadn't been interrupted. Like Bethany Clark, Connie's throat had been cut and her abdomen sliced open with several large gashes. The mutilations did not stop there, however. Upon examination, it was discovered that Connie Ballard's uterus had been removed.

I had the television on to the local news and listened to the reports while I tapped away at my computer, searching for dirt on Tanner Boyd. While I was interested in the murder of Connie Ballard, I didn't want to lose track of my actual job. Still, I found myself stopping every now and then to listen to some of the details. Once I'd had my fill of every record of Tanner Boyd's life I could bring up, I went out to get the morning newspaper to see if Connie Ballard's death had been reported yet.

She was on page four.

I was re-reading the article on the murder to see if I'd missed anything of importance. I hadn't. The young woman had been found in an alley. No witnesses. The police weren't going on record as saying this murder and that of Bethany Clark were connected, but anyone reading between the lines could see that they were going to proceed assuming they were. I was turning the page to find out what Bucky was up to in *Get Fuzzy* when I realized someone was peeking over my shoulder. Robbie had materialized behind my chair. He'd taken to wearing the sexiest clothes he'd had during his short life, and today he had on a blue mesh workout shirt that would have been tight on someone a size smaller. If he was trying to make me feel guilty over my dating decision, he was succeeding.

"I wasn't done with that page," Robbie said.

"I was." I avoided looking at him. My libido couldn't take seeing him in that outfit and since I wouldn't be able to touch him, avoidance was my only option.

"Okay," he said, moving around to sit on the arm of my easy chair. "But did I read that right? The uterus was removed from the second victim?"

"You read right. Our mystery man is one sick fuck."

"And the first stripper…."

"Bethany Clark," I filled in.

"Yeah, her. She was killed in pretty much the same fashion."

"That's right."

"And this girl last night, her uterus was missing?"

"Not to linger over the gruesome, but yes."

Robbie looked thoughtful. He hadn't exactly been a brain in his lifetime, preferring athletics to study, so it was a treat to watch him use the noggin. "Jack the Ripper's second victim, Annie Chapman, also had her uterus removed."

I had to beam at him. He was, despite his hanging around after death, pretty lovable. Damn him. "Look at the brain on you!" I said. "How is it you know so much about the Jack the Ripper murders?"

He shrugged. "I did a report on them for English my senior year. I got a B on it."

"And you remembered all that?"

Robbie looked proud of himself. "It was pretty interesting stuff, I guess. Besides—blood, guts, and gore. Interesting stuff to a guy like me."

"So you're suggesting that the killer is copying the Jack the Ripper killings?"

"Stranger things have happened." His face lit up with a sudden thought. "What if they're not copycat killings at all? What if the killer is Jack the Ripper himself?"

I raised an eyebrow at him and wished he weren't so close. He really did look hot in that shirt, even if he looked ten years too young for me. Complications, complications. "You said it couldn't be a ghost," I reminded him. "So unless he's celebrating his one hundred and fiftieth birthday or something, I don't see how it could be him."

"Possession," Robbie blurted out. "Maybe the spirit of Jack the Ripper is inhabiting someone's body and is re-enacting his old crimes."

"Fun thought. Is that possible? A spirit that old?"

"Of course it is!" Robbie was warming to his theme. He shifted from the arm of the chair onto my lap, although there was no weight to feel. His right side went right through the newspaper so I tossed it aside. I get enough reminders that he's a spirit. I don't need him going through objects. "For all we know he's been floating around since his death, just waiting for the right person to inhabit."

"He's a long way from home if that's the case," I remarked.

Robbie shrugged. "Maybe he came to America after the Whitechapel murders and died here. Or maybe he's gone from person to person over the years, just waiting for the right body that he could take over completely."

"And why is that theory any better than the copycat one?"

"You yourself said that he was giving off some major psychic signals. That would explain your reaction to him."

I pondered that. He could have something. However, having him sitting on me wasn't conducive to clear thinking. "Would you mind moving?" I asked him.

Robbie looked down and a shit-eating grin spread across his

face. "Aw," he said teasingly, "someone still loves me!"

I stood up, sending my body right through him. It's not a pleasant sensation to pass through a spirit, but I had to get my blood circulating. "I never said that I didn't love you. Quite the contrary, if you recall. Tell me," I asked him seriously, "what do you see when you look at me?"

He blinked. "I see you, of course. What do you mean?"

"You see me ten years older, though. I'm aging."

He shrugged. "I don't even notice it. People age slowly, and you adjust to the changes."

"There are no changes with you, though. You don't age."

"I can't. If I could, I would, because I know it bothers you, but it's out of my control."

I moved my face as close as I could to his. "I know," I said. "It's not your fault you died so young." I kissed his lips or at least the area where his lips seemed to be. It's hard to tell if you've hit your mark when there is nothing solid with which to make contact. I felt a cold sensation on my lips, so I was touching some part of him. It could have been his chin for all I knew, but I always kiss with my eyes shut.

When I opened my eyes Robbie was tilting his head. "You haven't kissed me like that in ages."

"I know," I said. "I should do it more often."

"Wait a second," he said softly. He closed his eyes in concentration. Opening them again, he leaned forward for a second kiss. This time I could feel the brush of his lips against mine. It felt wonderful to actually be kissing him again. It took so much energy from him it was something we rarely did. I heard Robbie moan and felt his tongue slip gently into my mouth. My mind flashed back a decade to when I'd been in college and Robbie had been a pizza delivery boy. Our first kiss had been at a dorm party at Purdue. I still remembered that kiss. It had been as sweet as the present one.

I opened my eyes. Robbie had given all his energy and was fading from view. "Thanks," he said as he vanished completely.

THE trip to Wales had been successful but had taken much longer than Caleb had planned. Most of a year had passed before he returned to his home outside of London. The amulet was buried right where he'd always heard, but other challenges faced him along the way. Now that he had it, though, he wore it at all times. And the magic worked. He no longer felt the need for the flesh. He ate food like other men. He was... human.

Wearing his stolen clothes and using money he'd taken off his victims, Caleb first took a room at the Lion's Mane. No more skulking in crypts for him. The landlord had eyed him suspiciously but had grudgingly showed Caleb his room. After settling in, Caleb had headed straight for Angela's house. Boldly he stood on the front steps and knocked on the door. He felt some nervousness, but he was confident that Angela would agree to see him. Then he could tell her of how he had worshiped her from afar....

His knock was answered by Angela's mother. She looked much older, more haggard, and she frowned when she saw Caleb. "What do you want?" she demanded.

"I wish," Caleb replied in his best English, "to see Angela."

"She ain't here." Angela's mother showed no emotion. She'd apparently ceased to care. "Gone off to London. Likely living on the streets, I expect."

And with that, Angela's mother closed the door.

CHAPTER 19

BEFORE heading over to Ellen Boyd's, I caught the *News At Noon* on Channel 4 to see if there had been any further developments in the Connie Ballard murder. There wasn't much. Ballard had worked at a strip joint called The Golden Palm on the east side of town. Her body had been found several blocks away, and her car, which had run out of gas, was left on a nearby street. It was assumed that she had been walking to a gas station when she'd been attacked. There were signs that she'd been dragged into the alley where the murder had taken place. It had been in a fairly residential area, but no one had apparently heard anything. The news crew had descended on the scene, where they found a disheveled Lieutenant Carson, who snarled at the camera and said that a statement would be issued by the department later. Seeing the good lieutenant so flummoxed made me smile a little.

A mention was made of the uterus being removed from Ballard's body and how that echoed the murder of Annie Chapman by Jack the Ripper. Unnamed experts worried that this could indicate the killer was copying the Ripper crimes. Robbie, it seemed, wasn't the only Ripper scholar in the Circle City.

I gave Daisy a pat on the head before heading out to my car.

At the Boyd house, a girl of about six or seven answered my knock. She was wearing jeans and a pink sweater that was a little too heavy for the September weather we were having. When she grinned at me, she showed shiny braces on her upper teeth. "You must be the detective," she said, opening the door for me to enter. "I'm Kali." She spelled it for me.

"I'm Duncan Andrews."

Kali twitched her nose. "Have you shot lots of people? Detectives on TV are always shooting people."

"It doesn't come up all that often, but I've shot a few."

This seemed to make her happy. "Are you a good shot?"

I nodded. "I'm a lousy fighter, so I compensate by being a good marksman."

Ellen Boyd came out of the kitchen, still holding a dish towel. She placed a hand on her daughter's shoulder and said, "Honey, why don't you go outside and play with your sister?"

"I want to stay. I want to see if Mr. Andrews is going to shoot anyone."

Her mother flushed with embarrassment. "Mr. Andrews isn't going to shoot anybody. Now run along and play."

Kali headed out the front door, but gave me a last hopeful glance. Maybe she was hoping I'd take out my .38 and shoot the television. As I wasn't armed and I had nothing against RCA flat screens, that wasn't likely. I pointed my right hand at her and made a gun-shooting motion. She smiled weakly to show me that somehow I'd fallen short of her expectations. I never did have much luck with seven-year-old girls. Certainly not when I'd been seven.

When she'd gone, Ellen turned to me. "Tanner is off playing golf with some buddies. I was hoping…." She stopped, putting a hand over her mouth to stifle a sob. Composing herself, she continued. "He's been acting so strange. Ever since he actually saw the ghost, he's been so withdrawn. He refuses to even discuss the matter, like it never happened and…."

I motioned to the couch. "Let's sit down," I suggested. Reluctantly she settled at one end of the sofa. I chose an armchair next to her, which was close enough for me to touch her. I did, putting a hand on her knee. I don't know if it comforted her, but I felt the gesture must count for something. "Ellen, what do you know about Tanner's past?"

She frowned. "What do you mean?"

"Do you know that he was married before?"

Nodding, she said, "Yes, but that was ages ago. He was just a kid in high school. One of those things. Her name was Cindy. He got her pregnant and felt he should get married. It didn't work, although it took them five or six years to figure that out. They were in the process of getting a divorce when she was killed in a car accident." Panic showed in her eyes. "What does that have to do with what's going on?"

"I'm not sure," I replied honestly. I was going on a mere hunch, but I could swear that Tanner Boyd had recognized the blue ghost. If he had and the ghost had indeed been that of his late wife, why didn't he say something? The hairs on the back of my neck were telling me I was on the right track. I'm not certain why I was listening to these hairs. They were the same ones that every now and then insisted I buy a lottery ticket as I'm getting my groceries at Kroger's. That's the thing with hunches. People get them all the time but forget when they don't come true. It's only that rare one that actually happens that makes us go, "Ah! I knew that was going to happen!"

"Does Tanner have any photographs of Cindy?" I asked.

Ellen shook her head. "I don't think so."

"How long has Tanner lived in this house?" I already knew the answer from my research, but I wanted to see if she knew.

The question surprised her. "All his life. This was his parents' home. They died in a car accident as well, about a year after Cindy and Tanner got married. He was just out of high school. They had been living in an apartment, but his parents gave him the house in their will so they moved in. When Tanner and I got married, we talked about getting a place of our own, but Tanner decided he wanted to remain here. It reminded him of his parents, he said."

I let out a slow breath. "I could be totally wrong, but I think your ghost is Cindy Boyd. I'm sure that Tanner recognized her."

Ellen gasped, although I suspected this had already occurred to her. "But why would Cindy be haunting the house?"

I remembered that my hand was still on Ellen's knee. I removed it, feeling a little silly. "There are lots of reasons why a spirit stays and doesn't move on. Sometimes they can't let go of a loved one." Robbie Church, raise your hand if this describes you! "Sometimes they feel they have unfinished business."

She shook her head. "But I've been married to Tanner for seven years now. I've lived in this house all that time, and we've never had any paranormal activity until recently. Why now?"

"When your husband and your daughters used their spirit board, they opened up a conduit, I guess you'd say. They allowed the ghost of Cindy Boyd to come through."

Ellen's eyes watered up and a tear ran down her cheek. "What can we do?"

I shrugged. "I've got a friend who's a whiz at exorcisms. If you want I can ask her."

She couldn't look at me, but she nodded. "Please do," she said. "I'll talk with Tanner about this when he gets back." A frown crossed her brow. "Do I have to tell him that we know who the ghost is?"

"It would be best. I'd want him here for the exorcism, and we'll have to use her name in the ceremony, if indeed that's who the ghost is."

Ellen Boyd chuckled without mirth. "Oh, it's her all right. It explains why Tanner is in such denial over this, and why he's been so moody. When can your friend do this... this exorcism?"

My hand found its way back to her knee. I hoped it was to comfort her. I'd hate to think that my right hand was straight. "Soon. I'll call her this afternoon and get back to you."

She nodded. I removed my right hand, thankful that I was left-handed. I'd hate to have to try masturbating with a straight hand. It probably wouldn't cooperate. And then where would I be?

I left Ellen Boyd to her worries, thinking that I really needed to get more sleep. When you start accusing your own body parts of being straight, you know you're sleep-deprived.

I HEADED for Meridian Street. Janice Sanderson had left several messages for me, and I thought I'd see what she had on her mind. I also wanted to see how young Kevin was reacting to the news that his beloved sister wasn't dead. Hopefully the little prick was a bit more on the cheery side.

As I pulled into the long driveway, I saw that a lawn-care crew was hard at work, with two guys on large mowers and another working on the trim along the sidewalk and driveway. So much for my vision of Janice Sanderson, still in dress and pearls, pushing a mower for hours. It was a fun fantasy while it lasted. I parked and went up to the door.

The doorbell was answered by young Kevin. He had an iPod in his shirt pocket and ear buds shoved into his ears. When he saw me he pulled out the buds.

"Your mother wanted to see me," I said.

The kid nodded. "She's in the kitchen. The woman she has who comes in and cooks for us is off on Saturdays, so Mom thinks she has to make something. I'd just as soon go to Chuck E. Cheese."

He wasn't exactly bubbling over with happiness, but he was nowhere near as morose as on our first meeting. He allowed me inside but hovered around as if he wanted to say something more. To make it easier for him I kept the conversation going.

"I guess you know by now that your sister is alive and well."

He nodded, his lips pouting a little. "Yeah, but she's married and living on the south side. It's not like she's coming back to live here or that I'll see much of her."

"You might see quite a lot of her now, actually. She's probably going to need someone to tell her troubles to."

That made his face brighten more. He tapped at the device in his pocket, presumably shutting off his iPod or putting it on pause. "That could be," he agreed.

"What are you listening to?"

Kevin eyed me carefully, deciding how much information I deserved. "Jonas Brothers," he replied, his tone a little defensive.

I nodded. "You like them, huh?"

He scrutinized me further and came to the conclusion that I could be trusted. He lowered his voice. "I've got a crush on Joe Jonas. I think about him all the time. He's so fucking hot."

Wow. Not only could I be trusted, I was now a confidant. I favored him with a smile. "In my day it was New Kids on the Block. I had a thing for Donnie Wahlberg." All a lie. Actually, I never listened to New Kids, but a friend of mine was a huge fan. I mentioned Donnie Wahlberg because his was the only name I remembered. Telling the kid I had a crush on Emmylou Harris when I was his age wouldn't endear me to him, however. Plus I was about ten when New Kids burst onto the scene, years younger than Kevin. I just couldn't think of any other boy group offhand.

The statement had the desired effect. Kevin grinned broadly and started leading me down the hall. "I'll take you to the kitchen. You won't say anything to Mom about my crush on Joe Jonas, will you?"

I turned an invisible key into my lips. "Our secret," I assured him.

He flipped his head to get the hair out of his face. "I'd love to see them in concert sometime, but there's no way. I'd be the laughing stock at school."

I could hear kitchen utensils in the room ahead. I kept my voice low as well to ensure no one else could hear. "My advice? If you can, go. Fuck what they say at school. Be your own person. Ask Brenda to go with you. Then if anyone gives you hell you can say you were just going with her."

Kevin grinned. "That's not a bad idea."

"I have them every now and then."

We entered the kitchen, a large room with copper pots hanging on a rack over a preparation area in the center of the room. The refrigerator was big enough to stuff a whole cow into. Janice Sanderson was chopping celery at the counter. She was wearing a dark blue business suit. No pearls, but I still enjoyed the sight. She made an attempt at a smile when she saw me. "Mr. Andrews, so nice of you to come."

Kevin, who had been right at my side, was suddenly gone. Seeing his mother hacking away at a stalk of celery, I couldn't blame him. "I'll be sending a detailed bill in the mail, if that's what you're…."

She waved the words away. "I didn't want you here to discuss the bill. In fact, I want to keep you in my employ for a little longer, if possible."

I blinked. I'd located her daughter. What else did she have in mind? A missing cat?

Janice Sanderson set the knife down with a frown. "I had a long chat with Brenda last night. She thinks very highly of you, by the way."

"She's a very nice girl," I said.

Janice sniffed. "She's too willful. Getting married to that… that person. Quitting her job to make it harder for me to find her. She'll do anything to upset me."

"Having spent some time with them," I said, "I do have to say she seems to be in love with him, if that's worth anything."

"I very much doubt that. She just hooked up with the biggest lowlife she could find. And now that you've found her, she went and called her boss at that strip club and got her job back. So now she's married to white trash *and* she's a stripper! I tried to get her to consider an annulment, but she wouldn't even discuss it."

Good for Brenda, I thought. I figured I needed to get the conversation back on course. "You said you still might need my services?"

She nodded. "I'm sure you're aware that another girl was murdered. Another stripper."

"I'm aware."

Janice moved toward the refrigerator. "Can I get you something, Mr. Andrews?"

"Nothing, thank you."

She opened the door and helped herself to a can of soda. She got a glass out of a cabinet and poured. With anyone else I'd have thought they were putting on airs, showing that they were above drinking out of a can. With Janice Sanderson I'd have been shocked if she hadn't. I could also see that she was trying to find the words to say to me. She added a few ice cubes from a contraption on the refrigerator door and sipped. Finally she said, "I'll be perfectly frank with you. I don't want my daughter married to that boy. I don't want her working at a strip club. She's only doing these things to attack me. I love her, but right now I hate her, if you understand what I mean. I'm terribly angry at her, but I want her to be safe. With two strippers murdered she's not safe working in such a place. I tried to get her to see that, but she refuses to listen. She goes back to work at that place Tuesday night. I want you to take her to and from work and make sure she's safe."

I shook my head. "I'm a one-man operation," I said—well, one man, a ghost, and a friend who's a witch. "I can't watch over her every second. I couldn't promise—"

Janice cut me off. "I just want you to escort her to work for a few days, stay with her while she's there, and take her back home. I'll pay your usual rates. I don't expect it will be for more than a week.

The police are bound to catch this killer before too long."

I wasn't sure I shared her optimism, but I said nothing. I could see by the set of her face that there was more to her request.

She continued. "She trusts you. She told me she liked you... and something about your strange dog. She'll listen to you. I would appreciate it if you would talk to her and make her see that a marriage to that man is unthinkable. She must get an annulment."

I don't do especially well with those steely-eyed glares. My face isn't made that way, I guess. I tried one on her anyway. "Mrs. Sanderson, I will, if you want, take Brenda to work for a few days. I won't, however, act as your mouthpiece. Her life is her life. I can't and won't interfere with that. Besides, I'm sure she wouldn't listen to me. Like I said, she seems to really love Derek. That's his name, by the way." I'm sure she knew this, but I couldn't help but notice she hadn't used his name once. "You might try getting to know him yourself. He is your son-in-law."

The words acted like a physical slap. She recoiled, sinking against the kitchen counter. She placed the glass of soda down with a slightly shaky hand. "I don't believe that she loves him. She'll do anything to hurt me."

I shrugged. "You could be right. It's still not up to me. I can do the other part of the job if you want. That's up to you."

Nodding, she replied, "I would appreciate it. Like I said, I want her safe."

Janice Sanderson's eyes were sad. She was encountering a problem that her large bank account couldn't heal, and she was at a loss. I almost felt sorry for her. I softened my tone. "Have you seen the place where she and Derek are living?" I knew she hadn't. The south side of Indianapolis was a foreign country as far as Janice was concerned. "They're living in a small house with Derek's relatives. A lot of people—a lot of kids—in one tiny little space."

She stood up straight, frowning. "What are you suggesting, Mr. Andrews?"

"I'm not really suggesting anything. I know if I was in your position, though, and I wanted to make a connection with my estranged daughter, I might get them an apartment or something. Set them up somewhere nice."

"You think I should reward bad behavior."

"I'm just saying what I would do. I might have a few conditions to go along with the apartment, though. I'd only pay the first few months' rent. That would give Derek time to get a proper job instead of working part-time and off the clock for an uncle. I'd probably even use my influence to get him a position somewhere. That's what I'd do."

I thought for a moment that I'd gone too far and was about to receive a tongue-lashing to put all other tongue-lashings to shame. Instead she nodded. "I'll consider your advice, Mr. Andrews."

Maybe I was in the wrong business. Maybe I should be a therapist… but no. My own life was a mess, what with not having actual sex in a decade. Who was I to advise others on how to live their lives?

Still, people did seem to like to confide in me. After all, I now knew Kevin Sanderson had a crush on one of the Jonas Brothers. Maybe next Janice would be telling me of her deep and abiding love of Richard Dean Anderson.

Or maybe not.

CHAPTER 20

I WAS still pondering life, the universe, and Richard Dean Anderson (so much better looking older on *Stargate SG-1* than he was younger on *MacGyver*—giving hope to aging males everywhere), and driving toward the west side when my cell phone rang. I was right by a Taco Bell and felt in need of a snack, so I quickly pulled in and parked. After shutting off the engine, I answered and was pleased to hear Nick's voice.

"I bet you thought I wouldn't call," he said. "We fags are notorious for taking phone numbers and then not following up."

"Somehow I figured you as the exception to the rule," I said honestly. "I knew you'd call."

He laughed. "Sorry about bailing on you so quickly the other day. I really did have somewhere I needed to be. I was hoping I could make it up to you by making you dinner tonight. I make a wonderful spaghetti sauce. Takes forever, but it's worth it."

Robbie. No, don't think about Robbie. Just answer. "Yes," I said.

"Great." He gave me his address, which was an apartment building not far from the bar where we'd met. "Seven thirty sound all right?"

Even as the words left my mouth, I felt like a traitor. Then I rationalized. It was only a date. Not a promise of a romp in the hay. Nothing had to happen.

I wondered if I should have just done what most other gay guys would have done under the circumstances—hired an anonymous hustler every now and then for my sexual needs and just lied to Robbie about it. Honesty is a bitch that'll kick you in the ass every chance it gets.

I WOULD have to take Daisy to the park while it was still light in order to make it to Nick's on time. Being a Saturday I could count on at least a few people at Gustafson Park. Once Daisy started chomping the heads off squirrels, I could count on *fewer* people at the park, but I didn't really want to cause a scene. Still, I couldn't think of a place in the area that wouldn't have some people enjoying the day. I'd just have to try to keep her away from families enjoying the playground area. Nothing scarred Little Janie more than seeing a sweet little bulldog devouring Sammy Squirrel.

Robbie appeared as I was attaching Daisy's leash. He was dressed in jeans and a tight blue T-shirt with Nike's logo across the chest. "What's up?" he asked, a grin splitting his face. I hated to ruin his mood. I smiled back but he could read me better than anyone. His eyes showed his hurt before I even spoke.

"We need to talk," I said.

He bit his lip. "Yeah?"

I sighed. Heavily. Daisy looked at the door in anticipation, as if to say the squirrels weren't getting any younger. "I want to be honest with you. I've got a date tonight."

There was a Bergman-esque silence. "Yeah?" he finally repeated. He looked angry, hurt, and sad all at once. The angry would have worried me when he'd been alive. Robbie had been very physical in life, which was great for sex but also meant that his first impulse when we argued was to tackle me to the ground and use me for his wrestling dummy. I imagine that was the hardest thing for him to get used to once he'd died, the lack of physical contact. Mine, too, come to think of it. Otherwise we wouldn't be having this conversation.

"I don't know why I agreed to it. I wanted to take it back right after I agreed to go. It's just dinner at his house. Nothing will happen. I promise. I just...." I paused as Robbie crossed his arms, making sure his biceps were showing to their fullest potential. "Robbie, you can't hit me. What's the point of flexing like that?"

"Don't be so sure," he muttered.

I shook my head and dropped Daisy's leash. Walking up close to him, I looked down into his face. "You wouldn't waste your energy," I said. I didn't think he would, either, but only because he couldn't hit me with enough force to actually matter. If he could clock me a good one, I wouldn't take any bets. "Look, would you rather me lie and just get a hooker every now and then? I would think you'd want to know what's going on in my life."

"Not when it's about cheating on me, you ass!" He rolled his eyes. "Yes. Yes, I'd rather you lie and just rent a whore. I'd feel much better not knowing. It could be one of those things we just never talk about. We both would know it goes on, but we keep quiet about it, like every Republican president has done since time immemorial."

I blinked. "Really? You'd prefer that? Living a lie?"

Robbie nodded. "Yes. Well, I'd prefer to be alive and fucking your ass nightly, but that ain't going to happen either." He took a deep breath and drew in some extra energy. The air around me got cold as hell, but I refrained from shaking as he pulled me in for a hug. "I appreciate you wanting to be honest with me," he said. "Sometimes, though, you can be too honest. I never want to lose you, and the thought of you dating...." He didn't finish.

I rubbed my cheek against the top of his head. It was nice to actually feel his hair against my skin. "I'll cancel the date," I whispered.

"No," he said. "That'd make me feel like an ass. Just don't do anything stupid. Like fall in love or anything. Just remember that you're mine."

"Couldn't forget it."

We stayed standing there entwined until Robbie's energy gave out, and he vanished from my arms.

NICK lived in one of those apartment buildings downtown that looked like they'd been there in the horse and buggy days. It had been refurbished and was now a haven for Yuppies and other up and comers. The apartments weren't large but most had a great view of the city.

I found apartment 2D and knocked.

I had gone for the business-casual look and was relieved that Nick had as well. It had been too long since I'd dipped into the dating pool. I didn't want to mess things up from moment one. Not that I wanted anything to happen. I just didn't want to mess up my first date in a decade.

Nick's cat, a small tabby, also met me at the door. "That's Jasmine," he told me as the cat wove its way around my legs in an intricate pattern.

"Hey, Jasmine," I said, crouching down to give the cat a good scratch behind the ears. She seemed to like it.

Nick had a large wooden spoon in his hand. "I'm still putting the finishing touches on dinner. Make yourself comfortable."

Nick was a gracious host. I actually began to relax and enjoy myself. He served the spaghetti, and we had some red wine, and the conversation flowed well. We talked of his work and how difficult it was to teach high school students, and we talked of my work, although I left out certain bits of information. The talk turned to movies, and we discovered we both had a taste for Peter O'Toole films and quoted our favorite lines from *The Stunt Man* and *My Favorite Year.* We started on a second bottle of wine and complained about reality television. We had just finished trashing *Survivor* and had started on another show when I had to put a pause on all the laughter and fun.

"Where's the restroom?" I asked in that hushed voice one uses when speaking of restrooms.

Nick took another sip of wine. "First door down the hall on the right. You can't miss it."

I rose from the table and smiled apologetically. "I'll be right back."

Finding the restroom was indeed easy. With only four rooms in the apartment it really wasn't an issue. I closed the door behind me and switched on the light. I had my zipper halfway down and was moving toward the john when I glanced into the mirror over the sink and nearly pissed myself. Robbie was reflected there, still wearing his mesh workout shirt and tight jeans. "Jesus Christ!" I blurted out.

"Everything okay in there?" Nick called from the dining area.

I gave Robbie my dirtiest look. "Everything is fine!" I shouted back. To Robbie I whispered, "What are you doing here?"

Robbie at least had the grace to look abashed. "Sorry. I couldn't help myself. I had to check this guy out. Make sure I approved and all that. I didn't want to be here and not let you know I was here, though. I didn't want to be dishonest about it. Not with Mr. Honesty."

I really had to pee, but if I stood at the toilet I wouldn't be able to see Robbie's reflection, and I wanted him to see the anger in my face. Peeing won out. I unzipped the rest of the way and hoped the sound of the stream hitting the water would drown out our hushed voices. "How did you get in here anyway? You've been in this apartment before? Did you follow me here?"

"Maybe not this exact apartment. I can't really remember. I've certainly been in the building before, back in my pizza-delivering days. And of course I followed you. What, did you think I just went from place to place looking for you?"

"You worked for a pizza place on the west side. It was nowhere near here. Surely they didn't deliver this far."

I heard Robbie chuckle. I wished he'd just appear rather than show up as a reflection, although I knew reflections took up less energy. I preferred to see who I was talking to. "Yeah, I worked on the west side back when you and I were dating, but during high school, I delivered pizzas for Poor Boy Pizza. They're defunct now, but they used to be right across from my school, only a few blocks from here."

My brain was wine-fuzzed, and I couldn't really think properly with the ghost of my boyfriend standing in the mirror while I urinated. The pee stream had ceased, so I lowered my voice even more as I tucked everything back inside and re-zipped. "I really don't think you should be here." I moved so that I could see him reflected in the mirror again. Robbie was standing with his arms crossed, which I'm pretty sure he was doing to show off his biceps to their best advantage.

The reflection smirked. "And neither should you."

He was being purposely annoying, which made me feel a little like teaching him a lesson. If Nick wanted a second date, he was getting it. I'd show my dead boyfriend he couldn't follow me on dates with the living.

"You okay in there?" Nick's voice was closer. He sounded like he was either just outside the door or a few feet down the hall. "Are you talking to somebody?"

I cleared my throat and quickly turned on the taps. "Just washing my hands. Be out in a moment."

"It really sounded like you were talking with someone in there."

"Just talking to myself."

Robbie's smirk went to Super Smirk. "Doesn't sound like the most trusting guy around. Want to hear my opinion of him?"

"No!" I hissed under my breath.

"What?" Nick asked from the hall.

I washed my hands quickly and scowled at Robbie's reflection. "We'll talk later," I said. When I opened the bathroom door I found

Nick waiting for me, somewhat concerned. He looked behind me and scanned the bathroom in the second before I switched off the light. He frowned.

"Turn the light back on for a moment, will you?"

I did. Robbie's image had vanished from the mirror, but Nick still poked his head inside and looked around.

I smiled at him. "I told you I was just talking to myself."

He shook his head. "It's not that," he said, puzzled. "Just for a second there, as you opened the door, I thought I saw a shadow behind you."

"Probably mine."

"No, there was some sort of dark shape behind you. I couldn't see it clearly, but...." He shook his head again. "Must have had too much wine."

Jasmine the cat had other ideas, though. She was in the hall, backing away from the bathroom slowly, with her hackles raised. Then she spun around and took off back to the living room. Nick watched her go.

"I wonder what made her do that?" he asked.

IT TOOK Caleb seventeen months to track down Angela. She had left London and gone to Paris, where she worked in a music hall, mostly as a dancer, but occasionally she filled in as a singer when someone was ill. Caleb got lodgings near the theater and attended several performances. She was much prettier than the other girls in the show and sang better as well. Caleb couldn't understand why they kept her in the chorus. He watched several shows and then, on a Friday night, decided to go backstage to see her.

CHAPTER 21

I WENT through the Sunday newspaper rather quickly. There wasn't anything new on the murders of the two strippers, although the paper was clever in re-hashing the same old news to make it seem like something was happening. More was happening with Odie and Garfield on the comics page, truth be told.

Daisy was snoozing on the couch, and Robbie was nowhere to be seen. The sun was shining brightly through the windows as I walked over to my desk and switched on my laptop. I sat down and did some searching to see if I could find anything online about the murders. There didn't seem much of interest and certainly nothing new. Google did, however, bring up a link to a serial killer site. I clicked the link, thinking what the hell. I wasn't doing anything pressing. The site was mainly devoted to Jack the Ripper, but other, similar killers were featured. There was a list of names, some of which I recognized, that one could click on for more information. Belle Gunness, who had murdered over forty people up in La Porte, Indiana, was among those listed. The ones who were never discovered or caught were listed by their crimes. One of these, listed as Showgirl Killer, 1910, caught my eye. I clicked.

The article I read was taken from several sources, mostly newspaper accounts. It told of seven showgirls in Springfield, Illinois, who had been murdered by "a knife-wielding maniac" over a two month period in September, 1910. Then I read a sentence that made the hairs on the back of my neck stand up.

There were some reports that the killer removed body parts from each of the victims. This was viewed by law enforcement officials as copying Jack the Ripper, who had removed several organs from his victims.

I leaned in and scrolled up to read more.

The Ripper had removed the uterus of his second victim, Annie Chapman. The left kidney and part of the uterus of Catharine Eddowes had been taken by the Ripper. Final victim Mary Kelly's heart was missing when her body was found, and her abdomen had been virtually emptied of its organs. The similarities between Jack the Ripper and the Springfield Showgirl Killer end there, however. Many reports claim the Showgirl Killer did remove body parts, but the liver seemed to be his favorite organ, as his third, fifth, and sixth victims were missing all or part of their livers.

My phone rang. I bookmarked the page and got up. The ringing had disturbed Daisy, who hopped off the couch and growled at the phone. I picked up the receiver.

"I hope you don't mind me calling so soon after our first date." It was Nick.

"Don't mind at all."

"Then maybe," he said with a little chuckle, "you won't mind me asking if you'd like to see a movie tonight."

Robbie hadn't been around once I'd returned home last night, nor had he shown himself at any time during the morning. I knew he was either sulking or avoiding me and thus avoiding being yelled at for interrupting my date with Nick. I had already decided to go out with Nick a second time, but Robbie's behavior made the decision even easier. "Sure," I said. "I'd love to."

I LET Nick pick the movie, which may have been a mistake. He chose an action flick, one with a lot of explosions, little plot, and cardboard acting. On the plus side, the popcorn was fresh and there weren't all that many people in the theater. Nick apparently liked to be approximately two-thirds of the way back from the screen and then as close to the center as possible. Luckily he found seats that suited his criteria, otherwise I'm sure a fight would have broken out. Most of the row was empty, but because of the location of these "optimal viewing" seats I had to plop down next to a skinny teenager with acne, who was stuffing his face with chocolate even before the coming attractions had started.

Nick gestured with the bucket of popcorn. I took a few.

"I've been wanting to see this," he said.

This was the same guy with whom I traded quotes from *My Favorite Year*? I chomped on some popcorn and decided not to worry about it. Everyone made cinema mistakes. After all, I actually *paid* to see Keanu Reeves in the remake of *The Day the Earth Stood Still*.

The lights dimmed a little for the coming attractions. The kid next to me moved his chocolate bar, and I could now see a familiar figure, sitting two rows up and about seven or eight seats over. He was facing the screen and paying no attention to us, but even in the dim light I could recognize the profile of Robbie Church. The seats around him were empty and no one seemed to be able to see him, but I still felt my temper rise. Was he going to show up every time I had a date with someone? Didn't he trust me?

The ridiculousness of that thought hit me. My boyfriend didn't trust me when I was going out and dating other guys. Did I really blame him? I turned to Nick and whispered, "Would you excuse me for a moment?"

He nodded. "You've got plenty of time. They usually run about ten minutes of previews before the movie starts. I'll save you some popcorn."

He obviously thought that I was going to use the restroom. I got up and pushed my way past the kid with the chocolate. When I got to the end of the row I looked back. Nick was engrossed in what was happening on the screen. Maybe he wouldn't notice me merely moving a few rows up. As quietly as I could I made my way over to

Robbie and sat down next to him. He didn't shift his gaze.

"It's times like this that I really wish that I could eat," he said. "An action movie really needs popcorn to make the experience complete."

"I'd ask what you were doing here, but I think that's fairly obvious," I whispered.

Robbie crossed his arms defiantly. "I wanted to watch the movie."

"And you just happened to pick the same theater that Nick and I were at?"

Robbie looked around him in mock amazement. "Is Nick here too? Maybe the three of us should sit together. After all, if you're going to be dating him I should probably get to know him."

I glowered at him. "You're being an ass. I told you nothing was going to happen."

"And I told you that I just wanted to see the movie. If you've got guilty feelings about cheating on me, don't take it out on me."

"I haven't cheated on you," I hissed. Someone shushed me. I ignored them.

"You want to."

"No, I really don't. I'd rather have sex with you, but that's not going to happen. If it helps, I'm not going to have sex with Nick, either. I just want to get to know him. I told you I wouldn't do anything unless I cleared it with you first."

On the screen, another trailer started. Robbie finally turned to look at me. "The thing is, you're assuming that this not having sex for a decade thing is only a problem you're going through."

"No, I don't assume that. We tried to have sex shortly after you died." I stopped and swallowed. That's not a sentence you want anyone to overhear. "If you'll recall, each attempt failed miserably. You can't summon up enough energy for something like that. It's just not possible."

"Not with a human, at least," he said, holding my gaze.

That made me pause. Repeatedly. "You mean... you can have sex... with... another ghost?"

He made a face. "Of course I can! And let me tell you, I've had offers over the years. I mean, come on. Look at these pythons." He flexed his muscles. "Remember that ghost in that house on Pennsylvania Avenue, when you were doing that missing person case? He wanted me *bad*. And did I cave? Nope. I thought of you and told him to fuck off."

I frowned. "He was an annoying little twink of a ghost that you couldn't stand anyway."

"Beside the point. I turned him down."

I looked around me. A couple a few rows up were looking back at me every few moments, obviously wondered who the insane guy was sitting there talking to himself. I sighed. "We'll talk about this tonight, okay? I'm going to go back and sit with Nick and watch the movie. I'll see you at home tonight."

"I don't get to see the movie?"

I ignored him and made my way back to my seat next to Nick. As I sat down he turned to me. "What was that all about?"

"I was just checking out that seat. Seeing if it was a better view of the screen." Okay, it was a lame excuse, but what else was I going to say?

I could see that Nick wasn't buying it. "You were talking to yourself."

I smiled. I was glad the lights were dim so he couldn't see me blushing with embarrassment. "I'm afraid I was being a very bad moviegoer. I was talking on my cell phone."

"I didn't see the phone," he said as someone shushed us.

"See how good I am? You didn't even notice."

Nick probably would have gone on, but luckily the movie started. As the opening credits began to flash across the screen, I looked over. Robbie was gone.

ROBBIE was on the couch waiting for me when I got home. Daisy was next to him but jumped up and came over to greet me at the door. I bent down and scratched behind her ears. She licked my hand. The place seemed ungodly quiet. I set my car keys on one of my bookshelves and went over and sat down next to Robbie.

I knew he had something he didn't want to tell me. After ten plus years with someone, even when most of those years that someone was dead, you get to know their moods. I didn't know exactly what was on his mind, but I knew it went deeper than a wish that I wouldn't fuck around with anyone else. He was acting so unlike himself, and I had been too wrapped up in my own worries to even notice. Robbie was nibbling on his thumbnail, something he always did when nervous. I reached over for his free hand. He exerted enough energy to make it solid enough for me to hold. We sat in silence for several minutes. I could tell he'd been crying, but Robbie was one of those guys who don't admit to ever crying. I'd learned long ago that if I saw tears running down his cheeks it was best just to pretend they weren't there.

"You know I love you," I said.

He nodded.

Suddenly it all fell into place, and I knew what was bothering him. "Who was it?" I asked.

He sniffed and cleared his throat before speaking. "There's this guy down the street. He died in a boating accident a few years ago when he was nineteen. You've seen him a couple of times. He likes to walk around the park at night."

"Gary?"

Robbie nodded. "I don't know what happened. We were just hanging out. Talking."

"When was this?"

"Back in February." Robbie sighed heavily. "I'm so sorry. It was just the one time. I was going to tell you, but…." He trailed off.

I squeezed his hand. Robbie closed his eyes and let out a sob. I leaned over and tried to hug him, but I guess his energy was waning. He wasn't solid enough to touch any more. My arm went right through him, and he vanished from my sight.

"It's okay," I said aloud. I'm pretty sure he could still hear me. Daisy came over, and I picked her up and held her close. I let a few tears of my own fall.

ANGELA was nice at first, excited that she actually had an admirer. When Caleb had knocked at the dressing room door he had imagined that Angela would be there alone, but she shared the room with several other girls. They graciously exited, though, to allow Angela some time with her gentleman caller.

Caleb lost his nerve, though. He got nervous and said too much. He told her he used to watch her at her house in England and that he'd followed her trail from London to Paris. He could see that his words worried Angela. Her manner grew cold, and she politely thanked Caleb and asked him to leave. Panicking, Caleb started speaking quickly, trying to show Angela his love was true. He said he wanted to marry her. She looked at his worn coat, his pitted walking stick, and his battered hat, and she laughed.

That made Caleb very angry indeed.

CHAPTER 22

I AWOKE Monday morning to a call from Ellen Boyd. Tanner hadn't been home, and she hadn't seen him since Saturday night. I told her I'd be right over.

As I dressed I called out for Robbie. Nothing. I didn't get the sense he was around at all, so I didn't think he was avoiding me on purpose. Most likely his emotions had drained him to the point that he couldn't even manifest. He'd be around later. I told Daisy to keep an eye on things and went out to my car.

When I got to the Boyd house, Ellen was waiting for me by the front door. She was pacing a little and didn't look like she'd slept at all. "I'm glad you're here," she said as I approached. "I didn't think I should call the police. I kept thinking he'd come in last night, but...."

I nodded. "How was he when you saw him last?"

"He was acting very odd. He's been withdrawn ever since we saw the ghost, but Saturday night he would barely speak to me. He sat at the kitchen table, just drinking beer and staring at the wall. He's never done that before. He didn't even talk much to the kids. Just sat there, drinking. Finally I got tired and told him I was going to bed, but if he wanted to talk, he could wake me up. When I got up he was gone. I haven't seen him since."

"Did he take anything? Clothes? Money?"

Ellen shook her head. "Just what he was wearing. His car and what he had in his wallet."

I gestured to the door. "Let's get inside. I'm sure we can find him."

I got Ellen to show me to the bathroom. She stood in the doorway while I went over to the cabinet. "Did Tanner use a comb or a hairbrush?"

She got that look that I often get from people who suddenly wonder if I'm operating on all cylinders. "A comb," she said. "Top drawer is his."

I opened the drawer and found a medium-sized black comb. There were several hairs clinging to the tines. "Can I borrow this? I've got a friend who can locate Tanner right away using this."

Ellen said, "Sure."

GINA was in her living room watching a DVD of *Casablanca* when I knocked at her door. The picture was paused on a close-up of Humphrey Bogart. We sat down, and she picked up the remote and shut the television off. "I've tried to watch that damn movie six or seven times now, and something always interrupts me. I've never gotten to the end."

"She goes off with Paul Heinreid, leaving Rick with Claude Rains. I'm pretty sure Claude and Humphrey walk off hand in hand in the last scene."

"Thanks. And Rosebud is the fucking sled. Now, what's up?"

I showed her the comb. "I need to find someone, a guy named Tanner Boyd."

Gina reached over and took the comb from me. She looked carefully at the attached hairs. "This one here is particularly good. It still has the follicle attached."

While I watched Gina got up and went rummaging through a small cabinet near the television. She uttered a cry of satisfaction and pulled out a small container. She sat back down and opened the tin.

Inside was a hunk of clay. It looked to be the same kind I'd used back in kindergarten. It even had the same smell.

"So what has this Tanner Boyd been up to?" she asked as she began to knead and mold the clay.

"His family has a spirit in their home. He won't admit that it's there, and I think the ghost is that of his first wife. He's been acting odd and has now disappeared. His wife hasn't seen him since Saturday night."

"That's not that long," Gina said.

"I'd still like to find him."

"He could just be freaked out from seeing the ghost of his dead wife. Not everyone handles the paranormal as easily as you do." Her hands worked quickly and soon the small mound of clay began to take the shape of a crude figure, human in shape. Satisfied, Gina took one of the hairs from the comb and worked it into the clay, making sure the hair was in what would be the chest of the figure.

"His wife, his present wife that is, is a nice woman. She's very worried. They've also got two young girls."

Gina smiled and got back to her feet. "Then let's find him, shall we?" She led me into her parlor, where she conducted her palmistry business. She sat down at the central table and lit a candle. "Would you pull the drapes? I'd like the room to be darkened as much as possible."

Once I'd closed the drapes Gina picked the clay figure up and stared at it intently. I stood by the window, more to keep out of her way than anything else. I also didn't like to be too close to Gina when she was casting a spell. I don't know what forces she called on, but whenever I was near her and she was doing some incantation or other, I felt chilled to the bone. I'm not talking about your regular feeling cold here, either. I mean like you've got a fever and the heaviest quilt you own isn't enough to stop the shivers kind of chilled. I hoped that by standing across the room I could avoid that unpleasantness.

"Little man, shaped of clay," she said, "I have something to ask of you."

The atmosphere of the room changed immediately. The room darkened as if the sun outside had suddenly been covered by clouds. The temperature dropped dramatically, but at least this time I just got goose bumps on my arms.

She continued. "We wish to locate someone. We wish to find a man named Tanner Boyd. I want you to lead us to him, little man. Take us to him, and don't fail us, man of clay. We must find Tanner Boyd, and we ask that you assist us."

I could hear some sort of whistling sound in the air even though the windows were closed and the air conditioner was off. There almost seemed to be voices within the whistling but they were too faint for me to hear any words. If indeed there were words.

Gina blew out the candle. A satisfied smile crossed her face.

"Do we know where he is?" I asked. The air was already getting warmer. I rubbed at my arms to get the blood flowing again.

She shook her head. "We don't need to know where he is. He is coming to us."

That surprised me. I had thought that she was creating some sort of locating spell. "You've summoned him?"

"And he cannot refuse to obey. He'll be here before long." She stood up and nodded in the direction of the living room. "Hopefully he won't come too soon, though. I'd like to finish the damn movie. I've just got to the point where Rick is drinking himself into a stupor, and Sam is playing *As Time Goes By.* Care to join me? I've got some tea made."

GINA finally got to see the end of *Casablanca.* As she switched off the set, she tilted her head slightly and scrunched her nose. "Movies are weird."

"How so?"

"That's supposed to be one of the great romances of all time, right? And she ends up having to go off with the handsome Paul Heinreid instead of staying with the troll-like, drunken Humphrey Bogart?"

"That's one way of looking at it."

She shook her head. "Don't get me wrong. It was good. I guess I just don't see what's so great about Humphrey Bogart. I'm not even sure why Claude Rains would go off with him at the end. Still, at least now I can say I've seen it." Gina picked up the clay doll that had been sitting on the coffee table while we'd watched the movie. "It's getting warmer. He's getting near."

"So it's sort of a homing beacon? A homing clay figure, so to speak?"

"Something like that. And while we're on the subject of romance, what's been going on with you?"

I told her about my dates with Nick and my talk with Robbie. "I can hardly be mad at Robbie, since he's been going through the same thing as I have."

"But he was giving you hell about wanting to start dating."

"Only because he felt guilty. It's a tricky situation."

"What do you plan on doing?"

I thought a moment. "I want to continue to see Nick. I like him. And I think he likes me. It'll just have to go very slowly. I want to make sure that I'm making the right decisions before I plunge into something. Insert your own dirty joke here."

Gina looked at me questioningly.

"I said plunge into something. I thought you'd make a comment. Anyway, I plan on being honest with Nick."

Gina showed surprise. "You're going to tell him you've got a dead boyfriend that you're still seeing?"

"No! I meant I'm going to tell him I want to go on seeing him, but that we'll have to take things very slowly. How are things going with you and the dentist?"

"The same. Slowly." Gina glanced at the clay figure in her hands and set it back down on the coffee table. "He's here now. Shall we meet him at the door?"

Indeed, a very confused looking Tanner Boyd was coming up the walk as we stepped outside. He was blinking rapidly, as if the sun was in his eyes, even though the day had become overcast. He was wearing jeans and a black T-shirt with a tear in it just over his left pectoral muscle. He hadn't shaved. I looked beyond him at the street, wondering if he'd walked all the way to Gina's. There was a car parked at the curb.

He came up to us, putting his hands up to his temples as if to stop his head from exploding. "I don't know what I'm doing here," he said. He looked at me and seemed to suddenly realize that he knew me. "What's going on?"

I don't know what Gina could see, but I could tell that something was very wrong with Tanner Boyd. His skin was unnaturally pale and his eyes had an odd shine to them. It almost seemed to me that something was moving inside his eyes, a sort of mist in the pupil. My guess was that Tanner wasn't alone inside his head. The spirit of his ex-wife (assuming that I was right in my guess as to the specter's identity) was in there with him. Tanner Boyd was possessed.

Gina took him gently by the arm. "Please come inside. You look very tired. You should rest."

He lowered his arms from his face and looked at Gina's doorway with just a little apprehension.

"I'm not sure… I should get home."

"We'll get you home," Gina said. "First, come in and sit down for a few moments. Duncan can call your wife and tell her where you are."

Tanner shook visibly as Gina guided him to the threshold. There he put on the brakes, refusing to go further. "No," he said, "I really must go home. My wife will be worried."

Gina was trying to pull him inside. I was behind Tanner. It was almost like watching a mime act with Tanner going up against an invisible wall. Something was preventing him from entering Gina's cottage. I wasn't surprised. Ghosts and witches don't mesh very well, so a ghost probably wouldn't feel too comfortable walking into the dwelling of a witch. I put a hand on Tanner's back and gently shoved. He lost his balance and tumbled forward.

As soon as he hit the threshold, he seemed to split. A howl that wasn't his erupted from his throat and a white vapor shot out of his mouth and nostrils. The mist went up into the air and nearly formed into a human shape before dissipating. The howl died away immediately and Tanner fell to his knees, breathing heavily.

Gina and I helped him to his feet. If he'd been confused before, now he was positively manic. "What the hell is going on? What's happening to me?"

"What's the last thing you remember?" Gina asked him.

He shook the cobwebs out of his head. "Last thing I remember clearly was sitting in my kitchen at home. After that, things are… hazy."

Tanner wasn't any too steady on his pins. Even with Gina helping to steady him he was leaning most of his weight on me. "You were possessed," I told him. "Don't worry. The spirit is gone now."

"Gone?" He gazed at me like I was speaking a foreign language. "Where? What are you talking about?"

Gina took charge. "Let's get you inside. You need a cup of tea."

Tanner protested, but I've never met anyone who could refuse to obey one of Gina's wishes when she really pressed. He sat on the couch in her living room and muttered while she prepared another pot of tea. Once he'd had a few sips he did look remarkably better. Some color crept back into his face, and he stopped shaking.

I sat next to him. "The ghost we saw the other night was that of your first wife, Cindy, wasn't it?"

He nodded. "I thought maybe we were just suffering from a mass hallucination or something. I didn't want to believe that she'd come back. It really was her, though, wasn't it?"

"Yes."

Tanner sipped some more tea. "And you think she possessed me?"

Gina was standing by the side of the couch, looking down at him. "We saw her. She couldn't enter my house. She's out of you now, don't worry."

"Where did she go?"

Gina and I exchanged glances. "She might be gone for good," I said, "or she might have gone back to your house. If you're feeling up to it, we can go and find out."

He didn't look like he was, but he came with us anyway. Tanner went with me in my car while Gina drove Tanner's. When we got to the Boyd house everything looked normal. A light sprinkle of rain had started and the temperature had dropped, but that was just Indiana in September. Nothing paranormal. Ellen Boyd met us at the door.

She hugged her husband tightly. "Oh my God," she said, her voice choked. I could see the tears starting to form in her eyes. "Where have you been?"

Tanner, still in her embrace, shook his head. "I'm not sure. I still can't think straight."

Once she finally let her husband out of her bear hug, Ellen smiled at me. "I don't know how I can thank you enough. I was so worried." She noticed Gina, and I introduced them.

Gina as usual was wearing enough jewelry to make an airport metal detector go berserk. She looked out of place outside a typical suburban house, but her manner seemed to put the Boyds at ease. "Do you mind if we come inside for a moment?"

Ellen ushered us all in. Gina sniffed the air and moved around the room. She caught my eye and shook her head. She wasn't finding any trace of the spirit in the room.

I filled Ellen in on what had happened. I purposely left things vague when it came to the spell that had brought Tanner straight to Gina. It wasn't that I didn't think they'd believe me. Once you accept ghosts as a fact of life, it isn't that much of a stretch to go on to witches. I did, however, want to keep Gina's secret from them as much as possible. From my explanation, all they got was the impression that Gina was a truly gifted fortune teller.

Once I finished, Gina asked permission to check out the rest of the house. She found nothing.

"This doesn't mean," I told them, "that the ghost is gone for good. Just that it's not here now. It may not come back at all, but I'd certainly keep an eye out. The first sign you get that she's back, call me. Gina and I can come out and perform an exorcism."

The Boyds nodded slowly. Ellen held her husband's hand. "Thank you," she said again. Tanner looked like he was going to be sick. He wiped a hand over his nose and stared at me.

I could tell he wanted to say something, so I paused by the door. He found the words. "She was insane. My first wife, Cindy. She was insanely jealous. That's where she was going the night she crashed her car. She thought I was having an affair with a girl from work. I wasn't. Hell, I barely knew the woman. That didn't matter to Cindy, though. She was going to confront her. She was speeding way too fast for the slick roads. It had been storming that night. The police say she took a corner too fast and crashed into a tree." Tanner Boyd sighed and slumped against Ellen. He was beat.

Gina touched Ellen Boyd lightly on the shoulder. "I can't feel her presence anywhere in the house. She seems to be gone. I think you're free of her. Just don't play with Ouija boards or anything like that and do what Duncan says. The first sign that she's back, call him.

We'll be right out."

We left the house. The rain had started in earnest now, and Gina and I rushed to my car to avoid getting too wet. Before I pulled away I looked back at the house. Everything looked quiet, but looks could be deceiving. I hoped that Tanner and Ellen were free of their ghost.

Time would tell.

CHAPTER 23

I HAD a few hours to kill before I'd have to pick up Brenda Sanderson for her shift at Pickin's. I was feeling a little weary and a nap suddenly sounded very good. Besides, I wanted to see if Robbie was around the apartment. We definitely needed to talk. Then I'd take Daisy out for her dinner and grab a bite myself. A greasy burger and some decidedly unhealthy French fries sounded good.

I got home in record time and patted Daisy as I got the feel of the atmosphere. Robbie was there, although he wasn't visible. I went to the bedroom and plopped down on the bed, still fully clothed. Just as I got comfortable the familiar cold sensation hit me, and Robbie materialized on the bed next to me. He glanced over at me sheepishly.

"What's up?" he asked.

I laughed. "Not much. Looks like I've finished with one case. Now I've just got to escort a stripper to work every night until her mother tires of paying me. How have you been?"

He shrugged. "Same. Want to talk about last night?"

"Not much to say. I'm not mad at you, if that's what you're wondering. I just can't believe you never told me in all these years that you could have sex with another ghost."

"It's not the easiest thing to bring up in conversation. 'Hey, did you know ghosts can fuck?' Honestly I never thought it would be important." He was quiet for a few seconds. "Sorry about ruining your date. I was being a dick."

"It's okay."

"He probably thinks you are bonkers."

"I'm pretty sure he does. I tried to get him to believe I was talking on my cell phone. I could tell he didn't buy it." I shifted onto my side so I could look Robbie in the face. "I'm going to ask him over and try to explain to him that I like him but that we need to just be friends for now. You okay with that?"

Robbie sighed. "You shouldn't let me... I mean, if you really want to... fuck, I don't know what I'm saying."

"It's what I want for now. I don't want a relationship right now. I already have one."

Smiling, Robbie stroked my cheek. He wasn't fully corporeal and it felt like I was being stroked by a feather. Still, it was nice. "I love you," he said. "And I'm so sorry for—"

"Forget it. I understand."

We lay there for several minutes. I wanted more than anything else to embrace him. To be honest, I wanted more than an embrace. Since that wasn't going to happen I sighed and turned onto my back and stared at the ceiling.

Like I said, I'm not psychic, but every now and then I get impressions. I don't know what triggers them, and they don't happen often, but when they do they hit me like a jolt. Suddenly I had a feeling of impending danger. Something was in the air, and it wasn't a good something. The only thing I had to do was to take Brenda Sanderson to work and sit there while she jiggled for salivating heteros. What could be dangerous about that?

Of course, there was the unknown killer who had already murdered two strippers. Was he going to strike again? My bones told me that it was a distinct possibility. And since the feeling of danger was directed at me, it could mean that he would be at Pickin's or in the vicinity, waiting for his next victim. I sat up.

"Robbie, would you come with me to the strip club tonight?"

He raised himself up on an elbow. "Is your Spidey-sense tingling?"

"Like it never has before."

"I wouldn't be able to go inside," he reminded me.

"That's fine. I'd just want you to hang around. Keep an eye on the parking lot, that sort of thing. Watch out for any suspicious characters."

Robbie grinned and pressed his lips up to mine. I couldn't really feel them, but it was a nice gesture. "Batman and Robin are back in action," he said.

While waiting for Daisy to chomp her dinner at the park, I called Nick. I asked him if he'd be willing to come over Wednesday night. He hesitated, not that I blame him, so I quickly explained that I needed to let him know what was going on in my head. He agreed to come. I did warn him we'd have to make an early night of it, as I'd have to escort Brenda once again to the strip club.

"Wow," he said, "driving a stripper to work every night."

"And back home," I added. "Makes for a late night."

"The life of a detective is never boring."

"Don't you believe it."

By the time I dropped Daisy back at the apartment it was time to go get Brenda. I never did get my nap. Oh, well. I drove to Gimber Street.

When I knocked at the door the sun was just going down. The rain had stopped, but the air had stayed cool. I wore a windbreaker which nicely covered my shoulder holster but wasn't really heavy enough for the weather. The door was opened by a blond boy of about fifteen or sixteen. I hadn't seen him before. I wondered if they had a steady stream of kids running through the house or if they just traded kids whenever they got tired of the lot they had. This one was wearing shorts way down on his hips so that his underwear showed. He glared at me. "Yeah?"

"I'm here to pick up Brenda."

He shut the door without a word. A few minutes later both Brenda and Derek appeared. "It's okay if Derek comes along, isn't it?" Brenda asked. She was wearing jeans torn at both knees and a big, bulky jacket with the Pickin's logo on the back. "He was going to come by later, but his car isn't working too well, and I figured it would be okay if he rode with us."

Derek smiled at me. "How's the zombie dog?" he asked.

"She's fine. How's the wound?"

He looked down at his leg. "All healed. You can't even tell there was a chunk missing." He pulled up his pant leg before I could tell him I didn't need the visual aid. The skin on his calf where Daisy had sunk in her teeth was still pale but otherwise unblemished. I told them I was glad and herded them to the car. They seemed to think it odd when I put them both in the back seat. They thought it odder when I explained that it was because my boyfriend was in the passenger seat.

As I started the motor, Derek laughed and said, "You've got a zombie dog. Are you also dating the invisible man?" Neither of them could see any trace of Robbie, obviously.

I glanced over at him. Robbie was wearing an old Mother Hubbard's Pizza T-shirt and a light blue jacket. I glanced in the rear view and saw they were both looking ahead, wondering what the hell was going on.

"This is my old boyfriend, Robbie," I said as an introduction. "He's been dead for just about ten years now."

"Ten years ago this October," Robbie agreed.

Brenda was looking around anxiously. "What are you talking about?" Some people could hear him or at least see a dark shadow where he was, but she wasn't one of those people. Neither, apparently, was Derek, who looked confused. I returned my eyes to the road.

"Trust me; he's here."

"You're saying there's a ghost in the car with us?" Derek asked.

Robbie turned in his seat and wiggled a few fingers at them. "Hiya," he said. There was no reaction. He shrugged and turned back. "Philistines," he muttered.

Derek leaned forward. "You mean he's right here? In the seat right there? Why can't we see him?"

"Jesus, I hate it when people talk about me like I'm not here," Robbie said. "It's so rude."

I knew he was kidding, but I wasn't in the mood. I spoke to the duo in the back. "He's going to keep an eye outside tonight. Watch for suspicious characters."

Robbie frowned. "Around a strip club? Hell, everyone walking in acts suspiciously."

"You know what I mean."

Derek ran a hand over the passenger seat, his arm going right through Robbie's chest. "Whoa," he said. "It's wicked cold right there."

"Would you ask him not to do that?" Robbie asked me. "It's fucking rude."

"It's cold because you just put your arm right through him," I explained. "Don't do it again. It annoys him."

"So there's actually a ghost in the car with us!" Derek was excited by the prospect. Brenda still just looked perplexed.

"I'm out of here," Robbie told me. "I'll be outside the club. If you need me, just pop out and shout." He vanished quickly before Derek could repeat his hand movements. Derek enthusiastically poked his head between the front seats to see if he could find any trace of the specter.

"He's gone now," I told him.

It wasn't entirely true. Just for a second Robbie's reflection showed up in the rear view mirror. He was flipping the bird in Derek's direction.

It took me quite a while to understand how ghosts actually move about. I suppose I was influenced by watching the Alistair Sim version of *A Christmas Carol* as a kid, but I assumed that ghosts could just fly around in the air like Casper from place to place. Not true. Vanishing from the car, Robbie would just be out on the street and would have to walk the rest of the way to Pickin's. Luckily we were close. He could do this invisibly to save energy, but he'd still have to make the trek on his own. Strangely, at his usual haunt—i.e., our apartment—he could vanish at will and just reappear in other parts of the house. When I asked him about this, he couldn't really explain why. "I think it's just a familiarity thing," he'd told me.

I didn't worry about Robbie. I knew he'd be there when I needed him. As always. I pulled into the side parking lot of Pickin's and found a spot. I got out first and scanned the area before I allowed Brenda to get out. Gotta earn my paycheck, after all. Everything looked fine. The three of us headed inside.

The same brawny guy was working the door who had been there my first night at Pickin's. I'd already talked with the owner and explained to him that I'd be escorting Brenda to and fro and that I'd be packing, so Brawny wasn't surprised by my shoulder holster. Brenda kissed Derek and started off to the dressing rooms or whatever they had backstage but stopped about halfway and darted back.

"I forgot to tell you," she said to me, taking my hand in hers and squeezing it. "Mom's getting us an apartment. We're moving into the Whitcomb Towers this week. Isn't that fantastic!"

I guess Ma Sanderson had listened to my advice after all. Maybe I should change my name to Dr. Joyce Brothers. "That's great," I said.

"We get the keys Wednesday. I can't wait. Our own place! I'm taking tomorrow night off so we can pack, so you don't have to pick me up." Brenda realized she was still holding my hand and let it go with an embarrassed look. "I think we owe you quite a lot, Mr. Duncan Andrews."

I just smiled. Brenda gave me a quick peck on the cheek and

then scampered off.

The crowd that night was on the thin side, and most of the guys were clumped around the areas where the girls danced. Most of the tables were vacant, so I picked one of those and sat down. Derek sat with me. The guy at the table nearest us had passed out with his head on the table, lying in a pool of his own sick. No one seemed to be with him, and no one showed any inclination to help him. Neither did Derek or I, to be honest, so I shouldn't cast aspersions.

After a bit Brenda's stage name was announced, and she came out to take her place on the bar. Derek beamed. "She's pretty, ain't she?"

"Pretty as a picture." The busty waitress came over. Or was she a bar maid? Whatever. Since I was working, I ordered a Diet Pepsi. It was going to be a long night. I hated the music, I hated the dancing, and I didn't have anything to say to Derek. I made a mental note to get a book of crossword puzzles to bring with me next time.

A little later the several Diets I'd had ganged up on me and a journey to the restroom was in order. I told Derek to keep an eye on Brenda and moseyed over to the men's room. The men's room was crowded and filthy. Most of the floor seemed to be covered in urine. The walls were painted dark to hide (unsuccessfully) the grime. Two overhead lights were out, giving the restroom an odd ambiance. The dark walls and dim lighting made it seem like how I've always imagined an English gentleman's club to be. Well, one that had been peed all over.

Luckily one urinal was free. I stood and did my business, looking ahead at a small frosted window that was slightly above eye level. As I was finishing I heard a muffled voice come from the other side of the window. "Duncan! Can you hear me?" It was Robbie.

I would have answered, but I was reluctant to cause the men on either side of me to believe I'd lost my mind. For their part, they seemed not to have heard Robbie's voice. I myself wondered how he had known I was standing there.

"Tap on the window if you can hear me," Robbie said.

I tried to reach up as casually as possible. I attempted to make it look like I was stretching. I rapped my signet ring twice on the glass. The guy to my left flashed me a worried look before he hurried away from the urinals. He must have thought I was a cop signaling for the place to be raided. He didn't even bother to zip up.

"I read you," Robbie said. "I need you to meet me outside ASAP."

I returned to the table. I leaned down so I wouldn't have to shout at Derek over the music. "I need you to keep an eye on Brenda. Robbie needs me outside for something."

Derek had had several beers by this point, but his eyes were clear, and he seemed alert. He nodded. "Be careful," he said.

I went outside and circled the building. It was fairly quiet except for two drunks who were helping each other to their car in the side parking lot. I wondered which was going to attempt to drive and then realized it wouldn't matter. They'd either end up splattered across their windshield or stopped by the cops. Hopefully the latter.

I found Robbie around back, near the frosted restroom window. He was hopping from foot to foot in anticipation of my arrival. When I got close enough to hear, he said, "I saw the killer!"

"Where?"

He pointed. Behind Pickin's was a long, dark alley. On one side was the back of a small, mostly disused strip mall, and on the other side was a fenced-in storage facility. "Down there. A guy in black was lurking around. I got as close as I could and—get this—he could see me! I mean, he turned and snarled at me! He freaking *snarled* at me!"

"When was this?"

Robbie had to force himself to slow his words down so that he was comprehensible. "Just a few minutes ago. He was dressed in black, taller than me, and had one of those pockmarked faces. You know, like he'd had smallpox or something when he'd been a kid. There was also a nasty, gross-looking scab on his cheek. That street lamp at the end of the alley showed his face clearly. I could see the pus in the wound! It was so…."

Now wasn't the time for the play by play report. "Where did he go?" I asked.

Robbie pointed. "Soon as he saw me he took off down the alley."

I moved, making my way quickly but cautiously down the alley. The night was quiet save for the chirping of some kind of insect. Robbie kept up with me, but only with effort. Because of the energy he was expending, just his head and torso were visible. He looked odd bobbing about in mid-air with only part of him there. I couldn't worry about him, though. My senses were reaching out for any sign of our mysterious killer. I was getting the faintest of traces, but that was about all. The killer had been down the alley, but I felt that he had moved on now and was far away. When we got to the end of the alley which opened onto a side street in a residential neighborhood, I felt we'd lost our quarry. I was getting no sense of anything out of the ordinary. Either he was long gone, or my Spidey-sense had conked out. There was a dog barking somewhere nearby, angered at the noise we were making, but no other sounds. I stopped and looked around. Columbo would have found a fragment of the killer's clothing snagged onto a nearby bush or something. I couldn't see squat. I looked at Robbie. "Any ideas?"

He was now just a faint face floating in the air. His head moved a little, and I think he was shrugging. It's hard to tell a shrug when you can't see shoulders. "Do you think he circled around or something? Maybe he's back at the strip club."

I tried to get the geography of the area into my head. The side street we were on must be Winton. "There's another strip club around here, isn't there?" I asked. "Over on Crawfordsville Road?"

"Don't know. Strip clubs aren't really my area of expertise." Even his voice was getting faint. Poor kid. He was on his last reserves.

"Why don't you go and rest," I told him. "I'm going to track this bastard down."

His dark eyes looked worried. "Be careful."

"I will be."

His face became a thin white mist which quickly dissipated. I got out my cell phone and called the operator. I told her I needed the name and address of a strip club on Crawfordsville Road. I expected a delay or at least some questions, but she came up with the goods right away. Maybe she was fan of strip clubs. I was committing the address to memory when something caught my eye. The alley I was in bisected another alley that ran behind a row of houses. A small garage faced me and in front of the garage was a dark shape. I had noticed it previously but hadn't given it much thought, assuming it was just an oil stain or something. Now as I took a better look I could see that it resembled a huddled shape. I disconnected with the operator and walked over. There was a massive stain, all right, but it wasn't oil. It was blood. And the huddled form was a woman's body.

The blood looked black in the moonlight and there was a hell of a lot of it. So much, in fact, that it was difficult to see any details of the victim. It was a woman in her middle to late twenties. She had been a redhead. Beyond that I couldn't say. Her clothes were for the most part sliced away as were large portions of her skin. The killer had done his job well. The abdomen was gutted, and she had a gash extending up from the sternum to her throat, which was also slashed. From what I could see it looked like most of her intestines had been pulled out. The end result did not look human.

I called 911.

I LEFT the tip anonymously, partly because I didn't want to be a witness to a second murder. Lieutenant Carson may have a soft spot in his heart for me, but even he wouldn't be able to keep me from spending all night at the police station answering questions. Also I wanted to catch the bastard, if I could, and I didn't want to be slowed down. I backtracked a little and got out of the alley. A short walk brought me to Crawfordsville Road. I was only a block or so away from the Winner's Barn, the strip club the operator had told me about. My brain felt like it was on fire. My hunch that the killer would strike tonight had come true, so I was sticking to my hunches. And my hunches were telling me to head to this club. It was a long shot, but if I was wrong who cared? Hell, I'd come across two freshly sliced corpses in the last week or so. Who else could make that claim?

The Winner's Barn (so named due to the proximity to the Indianapolis Speedway and the shape of the building itself) was set back a bit from the road. Their sound system must have been a beaut. Even at the far edge of the parking lot I could hear the thump thump of the music. The lot was about three-quarters full. Four guys of college age were heading inside. Other than that I could see no one.

I started to circle the building, looking for any mysterious shadows or, better, some guy dressed in black with a bloody knife in his hands. I found a stray dog sniffing around a trash Dumpster, but it ran off when I approached. The air conditioning unit on the roof of the Winner's Barn was making quite a din. A loose belt or something was making an ear-splitting whine. A scream wouldn't be heard by anyone inside. Not that there was anyone but me around to scream.

I looked around, hoping to catch a trace of movement to investigate. Nothing. Finally I decided to give up and headed back around to the front entrance. My shoulders slumped a little. Apparently my Spidey-sense wasn't as fine-tuned as I thought. As I rounded the corner to the front I saw a woman standing by the curb on Crawfordsville getting ready to open the passenger door of a black sedan. The way she was peering into the window sent warning bells jangling in my brain. Everything about her body language told me she was accepting a ride from a stranger. And my Spidey-sense told me this wasn't a stranger one could feel safe accepting a ride from.

I pulled my gun out of the holster and flicked off the safety. I kept it down by my side out of sight just in case I was wrong. "Excuse me, miss," I called out. I was walking fast but still had half the parking lot to traverse.

The woman, who was black and had the biggest afro I'd ever seen, turned to glare at me. She had opened the door and still had her hand on the handle. I was close enough now to see the dark shape of the driver. He had lowered his head to get a good look at me. I brought my .38 into view, just in case.

The driver suddenly accelerated. The woman yanked her hand away with a yelp as the passenger door swung shut. I ran the last few yards and fired a shot, aiming for the rear tires. My second shot put a hole in the rear windshield. The car's brakes screamed as the driver maneuvered a rapid U-turn. I thought for a moment he was going for the woman with the intent to run her over. The car veered toward me, however, jolting over the curb into the parking lot. The headlights were blinding, but I figured I had time for one last shot before the sedan would run me over. I fired and threw myself to the side. I felt the whoosh of the speeding vehicle as it missed my hip by mere centimeters. I rolled, intending to rise right back up, but I collided with one of those damn cement bars that mark the end of a parking space. With my rhythm totally off kilter, I scrambled to my feet just as the car disappeared around the corner.

The woman was not a happy camper. She was holding her injured hand, her eyes wide as saucers. "What the fucking hell is going on?" she demanded.

I dusted myself off and holstered my gun. "I just saved your life. Did you get a good look at the driver?"

"You some kind of cop or something?" The way she said it cops were several notches lower than cockroaches.

"Yeah," I said. The "or something" fit, so I wasn't lying.

She shook her head, making the big afro quiver like a mass of cotton candy. "I didn't see nothing."

I could feel a bruise forming on my hip from where I'd hit the concrete parking bumper and my windbreaker was torn at the elbow. I really didn't want to deal with her at the moment, but some extra info wouldn't be a bad thing. "If you could just give me a description of the driver—"

"He was just a regular guy. Brown hair. Looked regular, you know?" Her head shaking continued. "It was hard to get a good look at him. He was in the shadows mostly. Hey, I was just wanting a ride home. I don't need this shit. My car broke down the other day, and they want $400 to fix the fucking thing. It ain't even worth...."

She had more to say, but I stopped listening. If she worked at the Winner's Barn I could always look her up later if needed, although I doubted that would come up. I turned from her in mid-tirade and limped back to Pickin's.

CHAPTER 24

I WAS sitting at my desk on Tuesday morning, pretending to work. I felt like shit and ached all over and wanted to go back to bed. Three hours of sleep just wasn't enough. Robbie was standing behind my chair, his hands hovering over my shoulders. He was trying to give me a massage, but there just wasn't enough contact to really make a difference. It was a nice thought, though. Daisy was asleep under the desk, her body twitching every now and then as if she was dreaming of evil squirrels.

"I told you to be careful," Robbie admonished.

"I was. I didn't let the car hit me, did I?"

I'd had a busy morning already. I'd run the license number of the black sedan that had nearly run me over and got the name and address of the owner. I figured it was a stolen car, but it wouldn't be a bad idea to check up on it. If anything came of it, I'd have to let Lieutenant Carson know. I should anyway, but I was too tired to go over to the phone and dial.

That and the fact that I felt there was some supernatural element to these killings. The only time my sixth sense flared up was when some element of the paranormal was involved. Last night it had gone into overdrive. The police wouldn't be ready to deal with some supernatural killer. Neither was I, but I was going to try.

We had the television tuned to a morning news show. The lead story was about the latest murder. I twisted in my chair to get a better look at the set. A reporter was standing outside of Pickin's, looking very seriously at the camera. "Police believe that the murders of the three showgirls are linked. The body of the latest victim, Renata Brown, was found in an alley here behind Pickin's, a well-known west side nightclub." The camera panned over to show the entrance then came back to the reporter, who went on with his story. There was no mention of the incident at the Winner's Barn, so the girl with the afro hadn't said anything about our escapade, at least not yet. The reporter finished his bit, and they switched back to the studio, where the male and female anchors recapped the two previous murders. There wasn't anything new.

"So what now?" Robbie asked.

I looked at my notepad, where I'd written down the name and address of the owner of the car. Joshua Satterfield. The address was in Westfield, a suburb on the north side of Indianapolis. "I'll go check this out," I said.

"By yourself?"

I shrugged. "The car probably was stolen. I'll be fine. Don't worry."

"You said you'd be fine last night, and you ended up dodging cars and getting beaten up by a cement block. Let me go with you."

"It's up in Westfield. Not one of your usual haunts. Besides, you're still weak. I can barely feel your hands, and you're so transparent you look like a refugee from Disney's Haunted Mansion. Seriously, you go out like that, and you'll just be promoting ghost stereotypes." I thought I was being pretty funny, but Robbie didn't so much as crack a smile. The dead can be a tough room for a comic.

He stopped with the futile massage. "Just be careful," he said.

"Always."

A HALF-HOUR later I was hopelessly lost and very angry at Yahoo! Maps. Following their instructions I had traveled outside the city limits and had started down some country roads. I saw a lot of cows and a few farmers out in their fields doing whatever farmers do (farming, I assumed) but couldn't find the road I needed. Finally I turned around in a driveway and made my way back, thinking I'd get back to a street I was familiar with and try again. Maybe I'd missed a turn or something. Then I saw a side road I'd missed. There was no street sign. I turned. I couldn't get more lost.

About a mile down the road, the farmland gave way to woods. Trees lined either side of the road and provided a canopy, keeping out the sunlight, making the gravel road a prime candidate for an episode of *Scooby-Doo.* Then I came across a nearly hidden driveway. I would have missed it but for the mailbox on a post at the end of the drive. I slowed and checked. Sure enough, the number matched that for Joshua Satterfield's home. There was no name on the box.

I turned into the drive. The dirt drive wound around a bit, and I couldn't see a house. I had to creep because some of the pot holes were huge. Finally I had to stop moving entirely. I left the car in front of a crater that I worried would destroy the suspension and walked the rest of the way. I was wearing a leather jacket and my shoulder holster. The sun was out and the temperature was rising a little, but I preferred keeping the jacket on so that the gun was handy. I was out in the middle of nowhere, and who knew if relatives of those guys from *Deliverance* weren't hanging around the area?

My feet made soft sounds on the dirt. That was the only sound. No birds singing in the trees. I couldn't hear any critters rustling in the brush. Maybe they had more sense than me.

As I rounded a bend, I caught sight of the house. It was definitely a fixer-upper. The house was easily sixty or seventy years old and hadn't seen a paint job in about half that time. Some of the windows on the second floor were boarded up. On the roof was a weather vane. The wind was coming from the north. Good to know. There was a garage set a little behind the house with the door closed. All the windows I could see on the garage were missing the glass. Before going up to the house, I looked into the garage. It was dark, but I could see the shape of the car inside. It was the same one that had tried to run me over. Bingo.

I took my .38 out of the holster, put it in my jacket pocket, and kept my hand on it. No sense in taking chances. I went up to the front door and knocked.

No one answered. Where was this Joshua Satterfield? His car was in the garage. I knocked again, louder. Maybe he was sleeping. Maybe he was dead. Maybe he was undead. Certainly I needed to check. I tried the knob. The door was unlocked. If Joshua Satterfield was the killer, he was a very careless one. Or maybe he just thought no one could find him out here in the boondocks.

Inside the house was dusty and stuffy. There wasn't much in the way of furniture, and the few pieces I saw weren't in the best of shape. Obviously Satterfield didn't go in for the creature comforts of life.

I walked softly, but the floorboards still creaked every now and then. If Satterfield was home, he was deaf. I moved through an archway in the living room and found an old kitchen. The cabinets were mostly bare. Most didn't even have the doors on them any longer. There was a decrepit stove and a Kenmore refrigerator that had to be thirty years old. It worked though. I could hear the hum from across the room. Curious, I opened the fridge door.

Inside were several plastic storage bags containing some sort of raw, bloody meat. Nothing else. I picked one up. If I had to guess, I'd say it was a liver. Probably a human liver, not that I'd ever seen one before. Certainly I'd never seen one in a plastic bag in someone's refrigerator. And I'd certainly never seen one that had been partially devoured. I could see the teeth marks.

I tossed the bag back inside and started to shut the door. A sound behind me made me spin around. There in the archway stood a tall man.

He was slightly taller than me, so maybe six foot two. I placed him at 180 pounds. He was wearing black jeans and a black shirt. Not the most attractive man I'd ever met. Satterfield was clean shaven, but his face was wrinkled and scarred even though he didn't look to be much older than me. It was like he was aging too rapidly. He had something attached to a leather cord around his neck. Whatever it was, was hidden by his shirt. His eyes were heavily lidded and the bags under them were black and sickly looking. The whites of his eyes were bloodshot, and he wasn't looking at me with happiness.

"You're trespassing," he said.

I shrugged. "You're killing strippers and taking bits of them home to eat. Who do you think the police are going to be more pissed at?"

He started to lunge. I pulled the gun out and aimed it right at his forehead. He stopped in his tracks. Staring at the barrel, he laughed. "Do you think I'm afraid of your little gun?"

"I don't know. It's stopped you for the moment, so I'm happy. I take it I'm talking to Joshua Satterfield?"

He moved his head slightly. His dark hair was long and some of it had a tendency to fall over his right eye. The movement didn't help shift it much. "That's as good a name as any," he said. "I've had many names in my time. Caleb's always been a favorite of mine." He started moving, slowly, off to his right. He moved around me so that he was in the center of the room. He kept his distance, and I kept the gun aimed. I'll admit he really didn't seem afraid of my little gun. He was standing right in a shaft of sunlight, so he wasn't a vampire. What the hell was he, and would my gun be any good against him? I gladly let him command center stage. If he was impervious to bullets and attacked me, I didn't have an easy escape path with him blocking the archway. Now at least I could run like a coward and skip out the front door if necessary.

Satterfield was almost smiling. "You're the young man I tried to run over last night," he said with a hint of admiration. "You tracked down my license plate."

"Yep."

He looked down the barrel of the gun. "You might as well put that away. It won't do you any good."

His words had a ring of conviction, but I still felt better with the

.38 in my hand. "Want to give it a try?" I asked.

Satterfield tilted his head and stared into my eyes. It felt like my mind was being probed. I set my teeth and concentrated, thinking of only plugging him in his ugly face. His smile broadened. "You're something different. You know that I'm not fully human and the knowledge doesn't seem to surprise you."

"Not particularly."

He moved a step toward me. It wasn't a menacing move, but I pulled the trigger anyway. The bullet struck him dead center in the forehead and went through the back of his skull. Blood and brain matter splattered onto the wall and floor behind him. He went down with a growl and hit the cracked tiles hard. He didn't stay down, though. He got into a crouch and spun to face me, his teeth clenched. "That wasn't very nice," he snarled as he launched himself toward me.

It was like getting hit by a bulldozer. I didn't even get a chance to fire again. He was quick. He shoved me back, and we hit the kitchen wall. The collision knocked the wind out of me. I could still see the bullet wound in his skull. His right hand gripped my throat, and he started to squeeze. I realized the gun had flipped from my grip when he'd bounded into me. I tried to punch him in the face, but either I wasn't connecting, or he didn't feel the blows. The loss of air was making things go dark. The hand holding my neck was strong, and I couldn't break the hold.

The gun had at least affected him. The impact of the bullet had sent him to the floor like it would a regular person. True, he got right back up, even with a ventilated forehead and brain matter oozing out of the back of his head, but he had gone down for a few seconds. Maybe I could get another reaction out of him. Even if it gave me only a few seconds grace, it was better than nothing. I shot my knee into his groin.

It worked. He grunted loudly, bent over double, and moved back a foot or two, releasing the grip on my throat. I sucked in air and stumbled the few feet over to the archway. My head was spinning, but adrenaline and the survival instinct kept me going. I rushed through the living room, heading to the front door. I could hear him behind me. I didn't look back to see how close he was. At the last second, I decided I didn't want to mess with trying to open the door, so I veered off and ran toward the big bay window in the living room. I'd never thrown myself through a window before, but I knew what to do in theory. The answer is: don't do it. Shards of glass ripping me to shreds would only be slightly better than getting throttled by the intestine-muncher chasing me. I picked up a rickety wooden chair and used it as a battering ram. Glass went flying, and I leaped through the hole. I still felt some glass slice my skin, but I knew by the impact of hitting the ground that I was still alive. I was aware of blood running down my face, and I had to shake a large shard off the arm of my now-torn leather jacket. If this kept up, I'd have to buy a new wardrobe. There was another cut down my left leg, but it didn't seem serious. The scalp wound was on my forehead, and it was beginning to gush. With Killer Satterfield behind me, though, I didn't have time to worry about bleeding to death. I scrambled to my feet and bolted down the driveway.

My heart was pounding like hell, but I could still hear him behind me. He seemed like he'd lost some ground, though. His footsteps were further away. Maybe getting out the window had slowed him down. Good. I didn't want to tangle with him anymore. Something told me that if he got his hands on me again, he wouldn't give me a chance to kick him in the nuts. I wiped the blood out of my eyes and ran on.

Then I did the Idiot-Heroine-In-Every-1940s-Mummy-Movie move and tripped over a fallen branch. My face went right into the dirt, and I felt the jolt sing through my body. In desperation I grabbed the offending branch and threw it behind me. I think I had the idea that it would hit old Satterfield right in the puss, and he'd fall over dead because whatever the hell kind of creature he was could only be killed by a tossed piece of wood. Okay, it was a dumb desperation move. It didn't even hit the guy. He was further back than I'd thought. I got to my feet and ran on, rounding the bend. My car was just ahead. I pulled the keys out of my pocket and had them ready. My side had one of those pains from overexertion, and I was having a hard time seeing with all the blood running down my face. I got to the door and threw it open. Out of the corner of my eyes I could see old Organ-eater rounding the corner. I threw myself into the car and managed to get the key in the ignition without fumbling. I started the engine and threw the car in reverse just as Satterfield got to the car. He tried to throw himself on the hood, but I'd already started moving so he slipped right off. I ignored the pot holes and bounced and thudded around as I twisted back so I could see to make sure I was staying on the drive. Somehow I made it out onto the gravel road. The car slid a little, but I managed not to ram it into a tree. I threw the car into drive and sped off. Joshua Satterfield was nowhere in sight.

CHAPTER 25

LIEUTENANT CARSON didn't know whether to be angry or happy. On the one hand, he was furious with me for, as he termed it, "being a cowboy" and trying to catch the murderer myself. If I'd have just informed the police, he intimated, they'd have had Joshua Satterfield safely locked up. On the other hand he at least now had a suspect they could list as "someone the police want for questioning" in regards to the murders.

When the police arrived at the Satterfield house they found nothing to connect Satterfield with the stripper murders. Actually they found very little. The official statement I gave left out any reference to the supernatural. My private chat with Carson was more complete.

We stood out just in front of the house while I recounted my tale. Carson kept his hands in his pants pockets, nodding and shaking his head at intervals. Inside, a crime team was going over the kitchen. The blood stains in the kitchen interested them greatly. The story the rest of the force got was that I'd simply been nearly run over by a car and had followed up the license plate and checked out the house. When I'd found the blood stains in the kitchen, I'd called the police. I had hoped that they'd find the nibbled body parts in the fridge, but Satterfield had obviously taken those with him.

"So he's a zombie," Carson said when I'd finished. "Another fucking zombie." He glowered at me. "Why is it whenever you're involved in a case, it turns out to be some fucking monster? Why can't you just stick to divorce and missing person cases?"

"Actually," I said, ignoring his tirade, "it isn't a zombie. Zombies only eat living flesh. This guy took bits with him for consumption later. I'm not really sure what he is."

Carson rolled his eyes. "Well, that's one for the books. Something the great Duncan Andrews doesn't know." He looked back at the house. We could hear some of the commotion through the open front door. "Well, at least now we have a name and someone to look for. More than what I had before. There's no way I can link this up with the serial killings, though. Not yet, anyway."

I nearly felt sorry for the old bastard. I felt sorrier for myself, though. Before they took my statement the cops had a doctor look after my cuts and, while most of them weren't bad, the wound on my forehead had required three stitches. I'd have preferred to go to Gina and have her work her magic, but time had been of the essence. With Gina, though, I'd be sure there wouldn't be any permanent scars. Now my forehead would have a line over the left eyebrow for the rest of my days. I could only hope it gave me that rugged, dangerous look.

By the time they finally let me go, I had a headache and was starving. I had missed lunch, and my stomach voiced its concerns. I stopped at the first fast food place I came across and ordered enough for two people. A glance at my watch told me I didn't have much time before Nick was due at my place, so I rushed home to change. I thought about calling to cancel but decided I needed some supernatural-free moments with a regular human being.

I got home with little time to spare and quickly changed. I chose a pair of black slacks and a blue shirt. Everyone tells me that blue brings out the color of my eyes, which I've never understood since my eyes are hazel. I put on a pair of brown loafers as I sat on the edge of my bed. While I finished dressing I made faces at Daisy, who did her best to make them back. I wondered if I could powder the dog or something so that her fur and skin would look less gray and dead. Maybe I could get her some contact lenses for her eyes while I was at it and teach her to blink more. Who was I kidding? It wasn't possible to hide a zombie dog. Daisy gave up on making faces, sneezed, and trotted out of the bedroom to find a soft spot for a nap.

I felt a slight chill, and Robbie appeared on the bed next to me. He'd dressed for the occasion as well, wearing nearly the same colors as me, although he'd opted for a pale blue tie to go with his shirt. I disliked wearing ties myself, but Robbie looked smart in his. I told him he looked good. "Still, if you're gussied up for our guest, he can't see you. Remember?"

Robbie adjusted his tie. "Maybe I want to look good for you. Did you ever consider that? Besides, I think he'll be able to see me after you tell him about me."

I stood up, looking over myself to make sure I wasn't creased anywhere I shouldn't be. "I've already told Nick that I had a boyfriend who died."

"I don't mean that. I mean telling him that I'm still around. I think we should." Robbie noticed for the first time the bandage over my left eye. "What happened to you?"

I briefly filled him in on my adventures that afternoon. When I'd finished he stood up and embraced me. He was concerned enough that I could actually feel some pressure from his hug. He gently kissed my forehead, and it felt like an actual kiss. "I told you to be careful."

"I was. I used a chair to bust through the window. Not careful would have been either jumping through a plate-glass window and getting sliced like a ham or fumbling with the door and ending up as brunch for Satterfield."

His fingers brushed the bandage. "Does it hurt? How many stitches?"

"I'll load up on aspirin here in a minute. Let's get back to you wanting me to tell Nick about you. You're actually suggesting that I tell someone I have a ghost boyfriend?"

Robbie made a face. "If you're going to be friends with this guy, he's going to have to find out sooner or later. And I have the feeling that once he knows about me, he'll be able to see me. Just a hunch, but something tells me that's how it will play out. Where else were you cut?"

"Just some slight cuts on my arms and legs. Nothing bad. Tore my leather jacket, though."

"The one I bought you for Christmas that last year?" he asked, dismay showing in his eyes.

"That'd be the one. Hell, it lasted ten years. It was time to get a new one."

"But you loved that jacket!"

It was true. I did. Mainly because it had been a gift from Robbie. Further discussion was forestalled by the buzzing of the doorbell. Glancing at my watch I said, "He's a little bit early. Must be my irresistible charm."

Robbie made a face and vanished.

When I opened up the door, with Daisy hovering around my ankles, I found Nick standing there poised to ring the bell again. He smiled sweetly. "I'm a little early. I hope that's okay."

I ushered him inside. "Not a problem."

Daisy checked out the newcomer, her gray snout sniffing at his pant leg. Nick leaned down to pet her. "Hey, girl. How are you doing?" She licked his hand and looked up at him with her bloodshot eyes. Nick, getting a good look at her, nearly jerked his hand away but to give him credit he left it there for her to lick. It did tremble a bit, though. He looked up at me. "Is she sick?"

"In a manner of speaking. Actually, she's part of the reason I wanted you to come over tonight. Why don't we sit down?"

We both sat on the couch. Nick suddenly rubbed his arms. "Wow. I just got a chill. Do you have your air conditioning on?"

Robbie appeared on the other end of the couch. Nick glanced briefly in his direction but immediately turned back to me, obviously having seen nothing. Still, he'd had some sort of presentiment that something had been next to him. Maybe Robbie was right and, once the facts had been disclosed, Nick would open his mind enough to be able to see my spectral boyfriend.

I put a hand on Nick's knee. "This isn't easy to say." I took a deep breath. "First off, let me just say that I really like you. I haven't dated for quite a while, and I have to say I must have been waiting for you. You're a great guy."

He looked wary. "Why do I have the feeling that I'm about to hear the phrase 'It's not you, it's me.'"

"No!" I inched closer to him. "No, it's not that at all. Quite the contrary. Hell, who else would still be putting up with me after all the weird things you've probably seen?"

Nick smiled wryly. "Yeah. You do seem to like talking to yourself. And I knew you weren't talking on a cell phone at the movies the other night. So, what, you're going to tell me that you've recently been released from some sort of clinic?"

"I know a lot of people who think that I belong in one, but no. That's not it, either. You remember I told you that I had a boyfriend who died in a car accident?"

"Yeah. I'm really sorry about that." Nick looked concerned but still confused. He was trying to anticipate what I was going to say and couldn't come up with anything.

I paused, hoping that the right words would come to me. Should I just blurt out that the ghost of my boyfriend was sitting on the couch next to him? I opened my mouth and was stopped by the ringing of the doorbell. I excused myself and went to get it.

I found Tanner Boyd standing out in the hall, looking even worse than he'd been the other day. His hair was uncombed and a tangled mess, and he hadn't shaved. Desperation showed on his face. "I had to come and see you," he said, his words coming in a rush. "Something is happening to me. I think she's back. I think she's inside me!" He pushed past me to get inside, too upset to notice that I already had company. "I can feel her. You've got to do something!"

I looked in his eyes. Sure enough, there was the phantom mist swirling around his pupils. It wasn't as strong as it had been, but maybe Cindy Boyd was just in there conserving her energy. She didn't seem, at least for the moment, to be in full possession of Boyd. I patted his shoulder. "Hang on. I'll call Gina, and she can come over and do an exorcism."

I didn't really get the entire sentence out. Suddenly Tanner Boyd's legs seemed to give out, and he stumbled against the wall. His mouth opened in a silent scream and a stream of blue mist shot out of his throat. As soon as the last of the mist was out of him, Boyd slumped to the floor, unconscious. The mist quickly began to form into a figure right next to me. I saw Nick out of the corner of my eye. He had jumped to his feet, shouting, "Holy shit!" I didn't know if he could see the forming shape, or if he was just reacting to Boyd's collapse. Daisy, a few feet away, growled at Cindy Boyd as she rapidly took shape.

She was fast, and she was strong, much stronger than I'd ever known Robbie to be. Maybe, if Tanner Boyd had been right, and she'd been insanely jealous in life, her mental state gave her added power. Regardless, she reached out and took hold of my throat before I had a chance to react. Her hands felt every bit as solid as had Joshua Satterfield's and were just as efficient at cutting off my air supply. I gasped and tried to fight her, but every time I tried to connect with her my hands went right through. The only part of her that seemed solid was her hands, and I couldn't budge those. She squeezed harder, her screams of anger echoing in the relatively small room.

The lights went out. She was drawing energy from every available source. Daisy darted forward, teeth bared, but when she went to bite there was nothing for her to lock her jaw onto. I twisted in Cindy's Boyd's grasp. I couldn't see Robbie. Nick was still by the couch, his hands up to his mouth. He was crying out something, but the words weren't getting through to my brain. Everything seemed to be growing dark, and I wasn't sure if that was from oxygen starvation or the lights being extinguished.

Cindy Boyd's face was twisted in fury. She let out another scream and increased the pressure on my neck. I could see Robbie coming up behind her. He'd gone into the kitchen and was holding a cardboard canister of salt in his hands. "Hey!" he shouted.

She turned just as he opened the spout on the carton. Robbie swung, sending a fine spray of salt her way.

"When it rains, it pours, bitch!" Robbie yelled.

The specter's skin bubbled where the salt made contact. She screamed out an anguished wail before vanishing into thin air. Her howl lingered several seconds, echoing through the room. I fell back and nearly stumbled but managed to grab hold of the back of a chair. I held my throat and tried to suck in as much air as possible. It took a moment before I could get the words out, but I managed to croak, "When it rains, it pours, bitch?"

"It's the Morton salt motto," he explained. "Except for the bitch part. See?" He turned the carton so that I could read it. "I thought it had a sort of Bruce-Willis-in-*Die-Hard* ring to it. The heroes always say something pithy when vanquishing their foes."

I grimaced. "Yeah, you might want to work on that," I told Robbie.

A very white-faced Nick threw his hands up in the air. "What the hell," he asked shakily, "was all that about?"

I first went to the kitchen and got a glass of water. It went down all right, so my throat wasn't damaged. It was sore as hell, though. Nick followed and stood in the entryway of the kitchen. Robbie was standing right next to him, still holding the salt canister. I smiled. "Nick, this is my dead boyfriend, Robbie. If you can't see him, at least you'll be able to see the salt carton hanging in mid-air. My dog is a zombie, and I've got a friend that's a witch."

"Oh," he said in a very small voice.

I nodded. "That's pretty much what I asked you over to tell you. So, what's new with you?"

HE HAD killed her. Caleb had strangled his beloved Angela.

He hadn't even realized that he'd grasped her throat. Those minutes spent choking the life out of her were a haze. He vaguely recalled hearing her grunt and struggle as he squeezed, but it seemed more like something that he'd dreamed than an actual event. Her lifeless body at his feet in the dressing room wasn't a dream, though.

One of the other girls opened the door and saw Caleb standing over Angela. Angela's eyes were bulged out, and her tongue, purple and swollen, extended from her mouth. The girl screamed. The shrill sound brought Caleb back to consciousness. He pushed past the screaming girl and ran down the hall. He couldn't think. He just knew he had to get away.

And for the first time in ages, he wanted to taste some flesh.

CHAPTER 26

WHEN we pulled up at the Boyd house, it was a little after midnight. Gina was in the front with me. Tanner, weary and shaky, sat in the back. I had dropped Nick off at his place before going to pick up Gina. Nick's car was still outside my apartment, but I'd have to deal with that later.

The house was dark except for one light in the living room. Ellen Boyd was waiting for us outside and came to meet us as we got out of my car. Gina had a box in her hands containing a lot of candles and several spell bags. The box smelled heavily of sandalwood and rosemary and I'd had to unroll my window a little during the trip over to keep from gagging.

Tears had made a mess of Ellen's makeup and our arrival threatened to set the waterworks going again. She bit her lip and tried to compose herself. "Thank you for coming," she said. She began to lead us up to the house. "The girls are over at my mother's house. They're staying there tonight." She gave her husband a brief hug. Her hands felt the spell bag that was hanging around Tanner's neck by a leather strap. "What's this?"

Gina answered, "It protects him. While he's wearing that, the spirit cannot enter his body. It keeps him safe."

The Boyds led the way up to the house. As we walked, Ellen told us, "A couple of hours ago I started hearing something moving around in the house. I thought it was the kids playing at first, so I didn't give it much thought. Then I started to hear a woman laughing.

Right after that you called, and I got Mom to pick up the kids."

"Anything other than laughing?" I asked.

Ellen shook her head. "Not so far."

The timing fit. It had been a few hours since Robbie had dispersed the spirit with the salt. She had obviously gone back to her "home."

Inside the atmosphere was thick. Not only was she there, but she was pissed as hell, which wasn't really surprising. Salt and ghosts don't mix, and she was probably still smarting. The temperature inside was low enough that we could see vapor when we talked. She knew we were there too. I heard an odd murmur coming from near the fireplace. It seemed to emanate from the wall itself.

Gina set her box of goodies down on the coffee table. "Okay, let's work quickly. I don't want to give her a chance to retaliate. Tanner, Ellen, if you'd be so kind as to light these candles and set them around the room. Everywhere you can. Duncan, if you'd place one spell bag in each corner of the room I'd appreciate it."

The first time I'd seen Gina perform an exorcism, I'd expected a ritual akin to what I'd seen in horror movies, with bibles and crosses and holy water and beds levitating and what have you. She had explained to me that, as a witch, she didn't work that way. She used the powers of air, earth, fire, and water. She used the energy within her. It worked, so who was I to argue?

When we were ready, Gina turned off the electric light, and we were bathed in candlelight. She took her place in the center of the room and faced the fireplace. The Boyds and I stayed near the door. I was there to protect them, and I think they chose the spot so that they could bolt easily if it became necessary.

I heard something moving inside the wall. It sounded like someone was dropping a bowling ball down a staircase. The noise grew louder, and then we could hear a woman's laughter among the bangs and thumps. Gina shook her head.

"Cindy Boyd," she said, raising her hands in a commanding gesture, "I call you forward!"

The thumps ceased, but the laughter continued, growing so loud that it rang in my ears. Next to me Ellen Boyd looked terrified, tears streaming down her cheeks. If it wasn't for her husband's arm around her, I think she'd have run out of the house.

Gina raised her voice. "I can feel your presence. I feel your anger. I command you to show yourself! You cannot hide from us!"

A huge chunk of plaster burst out of the wall as if a charge of dynamite had been set off. Debris scattered onto the floor, and there was now a hole the size of a basketball about six inches to the right of the fireplace, right at eye level. Ellen Boyd squealed and clutched onto Tanner tightly. The plaster didn't fall far, so it wasn't like we were in danger of getting hit, but it definitely was startling. In rapid succession came two more bursts from the wall, making a line of holes along the wall coming toward us. A gust of spectral wind seemed to come out of these gaps, whistling in our ears and blowing Gina's hair back. Gina tried to hide a smile.

"You show your fear, and you have every reason to fear me," she said. She shot her right hand forward in a grabbing motion, clutching the air in front of her. As she pulled back a misty, blue-hued face showed in the nearest of the holes in the wall. The features were indistinct, but it was recognizable as the phantom of Cindy Boyd. The blue face was twisted in anger.

Gina pulled her hand slowly back, and as she did so the vaporous form seemed to be yanked from its hiding place in the wall. Soon the figure was standing in front of us. The ghostly wind picked up even more, becoming a howl in the enclosed space. Gina had to shout to make herself heard.

"You are not wanted here. This is not your home. I ask that you leave this place and go into the light. You will not be harmed. You will not spend eternity in hell. The light is a place of love and comfort. You need not fear it." Gina squared her shoulders and stared at the specter. "But hear this! You will leave these people alone! I banish you from this earth, this house, and these people!"

The figure was becoming even more indistinct and seemed to be shrinking in size. I could no longer make out any facial features. Now it was just a blue mist in a vaguely human shape. The wind was diminishing as well.

Gina went on. "Leave this place now and know love. Never return to this realm. You will be safe in the light. This I promise you!"

The form let out a cry and promptly vanished. The wind stopped at the same time, leaving us all staring at nothing but the holes in the wall. Gina turned to us with a weary smile. I could see the aura around her, and it had become a little hazy, so I knew she'd expended a lot of energy confronting the spirit. She acted, though, as if it were all in a night's work. "She's gone now," she told the Boyds.

Ellen Boyd looked hopeful. "Are you sure?"

Gina nodded. "Ghosts like that feed off of fear. Confronting them usually does the trick."

Leaving her husband for the moment, Ellen rushed over to embrace Gina. "Thank you," she whispered.

Gina patted her back. "My pleasure," she said.

IT WAS quite a while later before Gina and I got away from Tanner and Ellen. Gina had given them the rest of the spirit bags she'd brought and told them to place one in each room of the house. "Cindy has gone on," she told them, "and she won't be back. You want to make sure, however, that another spirit doesn't use her path to enter your house. The bags will keep that from happening. No more Ouija boards, though."

Once we got out to the car I asked, "What about Robbie?"

Gina was putting her seat belt on, and she waited until she had it set to her liking before replying with a question of her own. "What do you mean?"

"You said ghosts like that feed off of fear. It sounded like you meant the ghost needed the fear to exist. How does that apply to Robbie?"

Gina laughed. "Robbie feeds off love, you fool. It's your love that keeps him here. You haven't figured that out in all these years?"

I started the engine. "I guess I haven't really given it much thought." We were silent for a few minutes. I turned on the radio to have some noise. There didn't seem to be anything worth hearing, so I switched it back off.

"What if," I asked, "I ever stop loving him? What happens then?"

Gina shook her head. "That, my dear boy, will never happen."

TRAVEL was best. Staying in one place for very long wasn't good for Caleb. It made him think too much about Angela and what they could have had.

Over time Caleb realized that the amulet was flawed. Every now and then the magic seemed to wane, and he reverted to what he'd been before. After a few weeks of flesh-eating, though, he'd be human again. That was okay. Caleb liked being human, but every now and then he didn't mind enjoying the flesh. He gave up eating males, though. Now he just ate flesh from girls. Girls who danced or performed. Did that have something to do with his Angela? Caleb didn't know for sure. He just knew he enjoyed killing girls now. And eating some of the flesh.

It made him human.

CHAPTER 27

GINA had given me some salve to put on my cuts and scrapes, and once I got home, I applied the thick, slightly greenish mixture liberally and then replaced the bandages over the worst cuts. The one on my forehead that had required stitches was red, but the salve took away the sting immediately. Luckily my hair was long enough and hung over most of the bandage so it wasn't like I had a neon sign on my forehead saying "Hey, I've Got a Great Big Gash on Me!" The Boyds hadn't even mentioned it, but then they had other things on their minds.

Since I had the rest of the night off, I thought about heading straight to bed, but I decided to poke around on the computer a little bit before calling it a day. I'd put off continuing research on the Springfield Showgirl murders and wanted to see if I could learn more. Daisy settled at my feet and soon began snoring loudly. I felt a rush of cold air on my right side, and Robbie appeared, leaning against my chair and looking over my shoulder.

"Internet porn?" he asked.

I shook my head. "I found something the other day about a series of murders that took place in Springfield, Illinois, that were similar to the present murders. I just wanted to see what else I could find." I typed "Springfield Showgirl Murders 1910" into the search engine. I got 10,900 hits. Most were sites dedicated to famous serial killers and the first few I tried didn't have very much information about the Springfield murders. On my fifth try, however, I found that someone had scanned an article from a Springfield newspaper from September 19, 1910, concerning the murders. By then five showgirls had been murdered. The fifth murder had been witnessed and an artist's sketch showed the features of the person one Samuel Perkins had seen bending over the corpse.

It was a pretty accurate drawing of Joshua Satterfield.

"That's him," I told Robbie. "That's the guy out in Westfield with the fridge full of human McNuggets."

Robbie leaned in to get a good look. "Ugly cuss, isn't he?"

"And since that was 1910, he'd be at least a hundred and thirty years old now. Gets around pretty good for a man his age."

"So does Gina."

"Gina's a witch. I thought we'd concluded that this guy couldn't be a witch."

Robbie pondered this. "He's a ghoul," he said after a long pause.

"You also said he couldn't be a ghoul."

"Sue me. I was wrong." Robbie sat down on the arm of my chair. "Ghouls normally don't act that way. A true ghoul wouldn't attack a living person. They're scavengers. They normally just dig up recently buried corpses for their food. They're jackals. They don't bring down their own prey. They're too cowardly for that."

I touched the bandage on my forehead. "Cowardly isn't a word I'd use to describe this guy."

"That's why I didn't think he was a ghoul. The modus operandi wasn't right. This guy is something different, though. Something new. He's killing and taking bits of his food home to eat. Ghouls also don't generally live to be that old. They have a lifespan nearly the same as humans." Robbie grimaced. "Actually, they used to be humans. Eating human flesh can turn someone into a ghoul. It changes some people. Really changes them. They get so that they can only survive by eating human organs."

"How is it that you know this and I don't? I thought I knew

pretty much every preternatural creature around."

"Ghouls are all but extinct. I didn't think there were any around anymore."

"And you know so much because...?"

"Gina told me." Robbie smiled at me. "One night while we were watching movies. You'd fallen asleep, and the Bela Lugosi flick we had on couldn't have kept the most jaded movie critic's attention, so we started talking about stuff. I was mostly interested in werewolves, 'cause they're just cool, but Gina had some bee in her bonnet and seemed to think I wanted to know all about ghouls from A to Z. Glad I listened, now."

I looked back at the artist's sketch. The poor slob who came across the murder in progress, this Perkins guy, must have either gotten a good look or the brief glance he'd had had seared the image into his brain. In the drawing, Satterfield had a leather strap around his neck, but here his shirt was open, and I could see that he was wearing some sort of amulet. The artist had only given the bauble a general shape and hadn't filled in many of the details, concentrating more on the killer's face, but you could get the general idea. "That amulet. He was wearing something around his neck when I saw him. That might mean something." I started to click more keys but Robbie stopped me.

"You need to get some sleep. You've been running around all day. Jumping through windows. Dates with potential boyfriends. Exorcising ghosts. You're tough, but you don't have a red S on your chest. Go to bed."

"In a bit," I said, checking out another site.

Robbie put a hand over the keys. The touch was light, but I could feel his hand. "Go to bed. I'll do this. I've had all day to rest."

I looked at him in surprise. "You want to stay up and play on the computer?"

He shrugged. "I get on your computer a lot, actually. I've got to do something while you're away all day. Nice porn you've downloaded, by the way. I especially like the one with the skater dude with his arm in the sling. Some real artistic camera work on that one."

Feeling my cheeks flush a little, I said, "And you won't have any trouble hitting the keys? I don't want you to zap yourself doing this."

Robbie waved a hand in dismissal. "Piece of cake. I can let you know if I find anything of interest in the morning. Go on. I can see you're stifling a yawn even now."

He was right. I was beat. "If you're sure."

"I'm sure." He gave me a brief kiss on the lips. "I'll come in later and lie down with you. Now, off you go."

I went. Before long I'm sure I was snoring louder than Daisy could ever hope to snore.

I MADE myself a strong cup of Earl Gray in the morning to try to steam the cobwebs out of my brain. I sat at the kitchen table and let the heat from the tea play over my face. It felt good. It felt common. I needed more common things in my life. I loved Gina and Robbie and Daisy, but every now and then I wished I had an escape from all things weird. Maybe that's what I really wanted from Nick. Normalcy. Okay, normalcy and sex. I wondered what had happened to all my friends. I'd had friends that I used to hang out with, normal people who went to work, shopped, and didn't eat human body parts. What had happened to them? Why had I let them all slip away?

I sipped the tea. I could see Robbie, faded in the morning sunlight coming in from the windows. He was still sitting at my desk, but the computer was shut off. I suspected that he hadn't actually been researching all night, despite what he was trying to convey with his body language. I didn't feel like calling him on it. My mind was still too fuzzy. "Learn anything?" I asked.

He shrugged. "Maybe. It's hard to say. Kind of hard to really make out that amulet he's wearing in the drawing, so I didn't have much to go on. Couldn't find any other depictions of our friend, either. Best I can come up with is that it's some sort of magic talisman, keeping him alive. Doesn't look like 1910 was the first time our killer surfaced, either."

That woke me up. I set the tea down. "Really?"

"Eighteen ten. Stockholm. Seven girls murdered. All in September of that year. All had bits of them missing. The murderer was never found."

"Sounds like our guy." I rubbed a hand over my face. It helped a little. My brain felt clearer. "So your theory is that he murders seven girls every hundred years? Why?"

"Could be the amulet. It might be giving him an extended life. Maybe every hundred years he has to resort to eating human bits again to keep on living. That sustains him but only for a century. Then he has to re-fuel, so to speak."

"Could be."

"That first girl. Wasn't she missing her uterus?" Robbie looked disgusted. "He *ate* a uterus?"

"But eating someone's liver is okay?"

"Not as sick as eating a uterus. That's just gross."

I got up and went to the telephone. It took a few minutes, but I finally got hold of Lieutenant Carson. He didn't seem happy to hear from me.

"I suppose," he growled into the phone, "that you're going to tell me we're dealing with some sort of demon or something of the sort, and the only way to kill him is to chop his head off with a scimitar."

"Scimitars aren't easy to come by," I said, "so luckily that's not it."

Carson snorted. "Well, his name isn't Joshua Satterfield. That's for sure. Satterfield died a little over a year ago. Your friend seems to have borrowed his identity."

"And no sign of him?"

"Nope." Carson sighed heavily. "He seems to have vanished."

I told Carson about the cases in Springfield and Stockholm. Hearing about them didn't make him feel any happier. I told him that I just felt like he needed to know in case he ran into the guy. I also mentioned that we were going on the assumption that the amulet he wore had some magical properties. "That might account for his strength. The guy I met seemed to have the power of several rather annoyed elephants."

Carson thanked me, his voice dripping with sarcasm, and rang off.

Robbie frowned at the blank computer screen. He seemed lost in thought. "Something disturbing you?" I asked.

He made a face. "Not so much disturbing me, as...." He bit his lip. "I've never possessed someone. Not in all the years I've been dead. It just seems kind of rude."

"A bit intrusive. I'd have to agree."

"What if, though, you had someone's permission to possess them? Just for a little bit?"

"I'd think it would take an exceptional person to allow, willingly, a spirit into their body. Why? What brought this on?"

"I've been thinking about it since Boyd showed up here with Super Bitch Ex-wife in him. She was inside him, but he still had some control over what he was doing. He came here, after all."

"Yeah. And?"

Robbie batted his big browns at me. "I was thinking that if I was to possess someone that we could have sex again."

I was flabbergasted. Intrigued, I have to admit, but flabbergasted. "And just who do you think will go along with this stunt? Were you planning on putting an ad on Craigslist?"

"I thought about Nick. He didn't totally flip out last night. Okay, granted, he hyperventilated a bit, but once everything calmed down, he didn't run screaming from the apartment, vowing never to set foot here again."

"I had to drive him home," I said. "He barely said a word the whole way. Just mumbled to himself."

"Well, it's not like he was eased into it. He came over for a nice, relaxing evening with you and witnessed a ghost being zapped by salt. Could he see me, by the way? I didn't get a chance to ask him when he was here. After everything died down you bundled him and Tanner out of here rather quickly.

"Seemed like the thing to do. Nick was pretty pale, and I needed to get Gina so we could take care of Cindy Boyd once and for all."

"Did he say he saw me, though?"

I nodded. "He did. Just for a moment or so. I think when his adrenaline levels hit the roof something sparked in his mind. He saw Cindy coming out of Tanner, and he saw you with your little salt trick. Once everything calmed down, though, he didn't seem to be able to see you any longer. Sorry." I could see Robbie was disappointed. He hated that so few people could actually see him.

"Still," he said optimistically, "he allowed you to drive him home."

"He was shaking too much to drive himself."

"But he could have called a cab or something. I mean, he got into the same car with a guy that he'd seen a spirit come out of earlier. I think he has potential."

I chuckled, not really feeling any humor. "And you think we should now suggest to him that he allow you to possess him for a while so that we can do the hokey-pokey?"

Robbie grinned slyly. "It's worth a shot. Hey, I'd give anything to have sex with you again. I think it would work."

"I think you're crazy." I actually liked that idea, in a weird sort of way, but I didn't want Robbie to get his hopes up. "Although it would certainly make for an odd three-way."

"We should think about it," Robbie said. "At the very least."

I shrugged. "I do have to return his car today. I can find out how he feels about suddenly being thrown into a world with ghosts in it. He might have decided he doesn't want anything to do with me. Yesterday's shock has worn off by now."

"Only one way to find out," Robbie said.

I dialed Nick's number. He answered on the third ring.

"I thought you might be at work," I said. "Glad to find you in."

Nick sounded a little distant, but he replied, "I took a sick day. I didn't really feel like going in. Plus I didn't have my car. I seem to remember leaving my keys with you."

"You did."

"I seem to remember a lot of things. I don't suppose I imagined them?"

"Afraid not. How are you feeling?"

There was a pause. "Confused."

"I thought I could bring your car over. That is, if you want me to."

Again a pause. "Sure," he said. "But... just you, okay? I don't want any ghosts or demons springing out at me."

"Just me," I promised.

After hanging up, I quickly finished my tea and then fished out Nick's car keys. I was a little nervous on the drive over to his place, not knowing how he was going to react. Robbie had given me more to think about as well. I liked Nick and found him sexually attractive. If he went along with Robbie's little scheme, I could not only have sex with Nick but also with Robbie. I wasn't sure I could ever suggest such a thing, though, even if Nick was still willing to continue seeing me. Excuse me, but would you mind if my dead boyfriend takes over your body for an hour or two? Thanks awfully!

Nick answered his door wearing just some pajama bottoms. He hadn't shaved, and he looked tired. "Come in," he told me.

We sat on his couch. He offered me a beverage. I declined. The conversation kind of waned after that. Finally he said, "Do you need me to drive you back?"

"No," I said. "I can catch a bus."

More silence. Outside a bird was chirping noisily. Nick's cat jumped up between us. I petted it.

"So," he said, "the ghost I saw, the one with the dark hair...."

"Robbie. Yes."

"He was your boyfriend."

"Still is. He can't help it if he's dead."

Nick sighed. "I didn't get a good look at him, but he looked kind of young."

"He's been dead a decade. He was young when he died."

"And the dog?"

"She was resurrected by a friend of mine after she died." Another period of not much being said followed. I continued to pet the cat. It purred.

"So when you started going out with me...." Nick trailed off.

"Robbie can only have sex with other ghosts, and I can only have sex with other humans. It doesn't make for a great sex life in our relationship."

Nick nodded, a twisted smile crossing his face. "I can see where that would be a problem."

I told him about Robbie and how Robbie died. He listened attentively. I finished with, "When I started this, I didn't realize you'd get involved in all this supernatural stuff. I thought I could keep that separate. Actually, when I asked you over the other night I was going to tell you about Robbie. I was trying to let you know why I wanted to take things slowly. I didn't want to rush into something I'd regret later. I like you. I really do. But it's not fair to ask you to see me without you knowing about Robbie."

Nick was sitting a few inches away from me with Jasmine the cat in between us. He kept his face forward the whole time we talked, rarely looking at me. His arms were crossed over his bare chest which was giving me a "Don't touch" signal. Shame, because he had a nice chest. He coughed and then cleared his throat. "I like you too. I'm not sure how I feel about ghosts being around and all that, though. I'm going to have to give this some thought."

"I can't ask for more than that."

CHAPTER 28

I REALLY didn't need to see Janice Sanderson. I had told her on the phone that I wanted to stop by to fill her in on what I'd been doing. After all, I was still on her payroll, even if she was wasting her money having me shuttle her daughter to and from work. She could afford to be extravagant, though. I really wanted to touch base with young Kevin Sanderson more than anything. I felt sorry for the kid, cooped up in that huge house all the time.

I waited, therefore, until school let out before making the trek down her long driveway. Kevin answered the door. "Mom's in the living room," he said.

I stayed on the stoop for a moment and fished into my pocket. "Wait a second. I've got something for you."

His eyes nearly popped out of his skull when I handed him two tickets to a Jonas Brothers concert. "Are you kidding me?" he squealed.

"It's in Chicago, though. If you need a ride my friend Gina and I can drive you up there. If your mother approves, that is."

Kevin frowned. "I don't have anyone to take, though."

"I bet if you asked one of the girls in your class you'd find someone who'd kill to go with you."

He considered this. "Well, I guess I could ask Sharon Caldwell. She's a pretty good friend. And I know she likes the Jonas Brothers."

"There you go. You'll be able to see Joe Jonas up close."

Kevin smiled shyly at me. "Lately I think I like Nick Jonas even more."

"I like a guy named Nick myself. The show isn't for a few weeks yet, so you've got plenty of time to get someone to go with and clear everything with your mother."

He was beaming. Still clutching the tickets as if they were gold, he hugged me quickly. "Thanks. You're the best."

"So I've been told."

IT SEEMED to be a good day for Sandersons all around. I found Ma Sanderson in the living room as Kevin had said. She was reading a magazine but actually smiled as I entered the room. "So nice to see you, Mr. Andrews."

I shook her hand and sat down in an armchair near her. It obviously was made for looks and not comfort, but I wasn't planning on staying long. "I understand that Brenda and Derek are moving into their new apartment today."

"Yes," she said. "That was a good suggestion of yours. Brenda and I have had several talks lately. I still think she could do better than that sleazy boy she's seeing."

"They're married," I reminded her.

That nearly ruined her good mood. She shivered involuntarily but recovered herself admirably. "Yes. I suppose I have to accept that."

"Which do you dislike more," I asked her, "Brenda's choice of husband or her choice of work?"

There was no question there. Janice Sanderson answered without hesitation. "That place she calls work."

"Maybe you should get Derek on your side. After all, I don't imagine he's real thrilled with his wife getting dollar bills shoved into her G-string. Between the two of you, you might get her to start thinking of looking for something else."

Janice nodded. It was a slow, thoughtful nod, but a nod just the same. "Do you always dish out personal advice to your clients?" she asked.

"Only when they seem receptive to it."

She smiled at me. "You're a very perceptive young man. You see things a lot of people don't, I think."

"Oh, ain't that the truth."

I HAD to pick Brenda up at their new apartment. They were still moving in boxes and everything was a jumble. Derek and a friend with a pickup truck were making trips back and forth from Gimber Street. He wasn't there when I arrived. Brenda showed me around. It was a nice apartment, twenty floors up, and she was glowing with pride.

"I can't believe Mom got this for us," she said. Excitedly she pulled me over to the sliding glass doors that led out onto the balcony. "Wait until you see the view! It's spectacular!"

I had to agree. The whole of downtown Indianapolis spread out in front of us. Nice as the view was, though, I reminded her of the time. "If we're going to get you to work on time, we should be leaving."

The night had a little chill to it, so Brenda went to get a light jacket. As she put it on, she asked, "So what about the ghost? Is he coming with us again tonight?"

"Robbie? Yeah, actually. He's down in the car."

She seemed a little disappointed. "He could have come up. I could always say then that we've had a ghost in our apartment."

"He could, actually. He's been in this building before, but he wanted to listen to a song on the radio."

That amused her. "A ghost that likes music. How sweet."

I had to agree with her. Robbie was very sweet.

THE drive to Pickin's was uneventful. Brenda sat in the back, which may have looked odd to anyone pulling next to us at a light, but I didn't care. Robbie was listening to some classic rock but every now and then had to change stations when they played something he couldn't stand. Brenda enjoyed watching the knobs seemingly moving on their own.

When we got to Pickin's, I wasn't surprised to find a police car parked in the side lot. Either the presence of the fuzz put off the clientele, or it was just too early, because there weren't that many cars in the lot. Robbie stayed in the car while I escorted Brenda inside.

The doorman smiled at me. "Packing tonight?" he asked.

I opened my jacket enough for him to see the holster. Tonight the gun was loaded with silver bullets. Gina always kept a supply handy, bless her. I didn't know if they'd work against our ghoul, but I knew regular bullets didn't affect him, so I figured I'd give the silver ones a try. "Of course."

He nodded his approval. Brenda gave me a quick peck on the cheek and went off to change. I picked a table near the back and sat down. I wished I'd remembered to bring a book. Across the room I saw Craig. He waved at me. I waved back, but without enthusiasm. I didn't want him to get the wrong idea. He looked better tonight than I'd ever seen him. His hair was washed, a major plus, and he had on clean, new-looking clothes. I couldn't see his teeth from where I was but I figured they still needed some work. I was glad, though, that he was making an effort. He was a nice guy. He was still sitting close to where his sister was stripping, though, and that was just a little on the creepy side.

I had several sodas and tried not to continually look at my watch. The bar closed at three, and it was usually four o'clock or later that Brenda actually was ready to leave. Hours to kill. I played a game in my head, watching the patrons and trying to decide what their occupation was. There weren't many, so the game didn't last long. I decided there were two construction workers, a plainclothes cop (keeping an eye on the inside while his uniformed compatriot watched outside in his car), three accountants, and an unsuccessful poet. The others were in the shadows, and I couldn't decide on what they did.

Nothing was going to happen to Brenda while she was inside the building, so I took a little break and went outside for some air. I sauntered around and ended up at the side of the building. The night was overcast, and there was no moon, but a streetlight at the corner kept most of the parking lot visible. I could see that my aimless meandering had caught the attention of the cop parked near the lot's entrance. I waved at him. He was mostly in shadow, but it didn't look like he waved back. I could see he was staring right at me, though. I thought about going over and introducing myself but decided against it. Instead I headed over to my car and got in on the driver's side. I shut the door and sighed heavily. Robbie appeared in the passenger seat.

"Long night?" he asked.

"I don't know how much more of this I can take," I told him. "Granted, Janice Sanderson is loaded and won't miss the money, but she's doing nothing but padding my bank account by having me do this. There's a cop out here and at least one inside. Brenda Sanderson is safe in there. All I'm doing is drinking too many sodas and getting bored out of my skull."

"It's not like you can enjoy the scenery, either," Robbie said.

"Very true."

"Still," he said, trying to be optimistic, "stake-outs are dull too."

"Which is why I avoid doing them." I sighed. "Still, I'm getting paid. And the money I'll be getting from Janice Sanderson will help out the finances greatly. Hell, I might just treat us to a big plasma television after this is all over." I gazed out at the parking lot. The cop had lost interest in me and was reading a newspaper by the light of the street lamp. No one else was in sight. The parking lot didn't seem to have filled up any from when we'd arrived. The strip club business was waning. A series of murders will do that for business. "I sincerely doubt our ghoul is going to be showing his face anywhere near here, no matter how badly he needs to chomp on some organs. There are tons of strip clubs all over Indianapolis. He'd be a fool to stay in this area."

"Jack the Ripper did," Robbie said. "Stayed in the Whitechapel area. And even with extra police patrols they never caught him. Maybe serial killers have a comfort zone and don't like traveling outside their little area. Besides, you've met the guy. Did he seem like he was worried about getting caught?"

"He seemed like he wanted to choke the life out of me. Anything more than that I wasn't concerned with at that time." I closed my eyes, breathing deeply. It was much nicer out in the car with Robbie. The smoke in the bar bothered me. "I had Gina look at the drawing of the Springfield killer earlier today. She agreed with you that the amulet probably had magical properties. She also agreed that the sketch wasn't clear enough to tell more than that."

"A ghost and a witch agreeing on something. We've set a precedent."

"Why only every hundred years, I wonder?"

Robbie cocked his head in thought. "What do you mean?"

"Why does he only go on a murder and organ-eating spree every hundred years? If he's a ghoul, why haven't we found cases of him around the world, eating and killing his way across continents?"

After giving that some pondering time, Robbie replied, "The amulet. Hell, it does something for him. A bullet in the forehead would have killed a normal ghoul, so we know he's got something special going on. A ghoul good luck charm, maybe? Like he can't be killed while he's wearing it? Maybe the amulet makes him human, or at least less of a ghoul, for most of the time, and he has to re-charge himself every hundred years to keep things going. Both in Stockholm and Springfield there were seven girls murdered, all with organs missing. Mostly the liver and the odd uterus or two." Robbie made a face. "I still can't believe he's eaten someone's uterus."

"Seven organs from seven girls once every hundred years to stay human? It could be, I suppose. Why showgirls though?"

Robbie shrugged. "Maybe he just hates showgirls. Maybe he got jilted by one. Why did Jack the Ripper kill prostitutes? It's hard to say how madmen think."

"You keep on going on about Jack the Ripper."

"He's fascinating."

I decided to change the subject. "My chat with Nick went well. As well as could be expected, anyway."

Robbie looked eager. "Did he say he'd let me possess him? What did he think about that?"

I chuckled. "I didn't ask. Too soon. He's coping with finding out that you're in my life and that I've got a zombie for a dog. Asking him if he'll let you take over his body for a while so we can fornicate is a discussion for a later time." Probably much later. "He didn't run screaming, though. We're going to take things slowly and see what happens."

"It would mean everything to me," Robbie said, his tone serious, "to make love to you again."

"Yeah," I agreed, "me too."

I reached over for his hand. He concentrated so that I could grasp it. We sat like that for a few minutes, holding hands and smiling like new lovers.

AFTER a bit I re-entered Pickin's, mainly because I had to pee. Brawny the bouncer nodded at me as I went past. He looked as bored as I was. I made straight for the restroom. No one was using the facilities, but I still went to the center urinal, the one under the window. Maybe I had a comfort zone where urinals were concerned. I did my business and then went to wash up. As soon as the water hit my hands I felt my senses go into overdrive. It hit me like an electric shock, and I actually shuddered and stepped back a few paces, my first thought being that the water had caused the sensory overload. Once I caught my breath I realized that was stupid. My Spidey-sense only worked, when it decided to work, when something paranormal was nearby. It had never been this strong, though. I didn't know what that meant, but I figured it wasn't good. I quickly dried my hands and left the restroom.

At first glance everything looked normal. The girls were dancing. The few guys at the bar seemed to be enjoying the show. A few were even tucking bills into the girls' G-strings. Brenda was in her usual spot, dancing away. Her old roommate, Tiffany, was near her on the bar, with brother Craig sitting close by. Then I looked over at the door where Brawny was stationed.

He was dealing with a tall man dressed in black who'd just entered. They seemed to be having words. The man was wearing a long leather coat and, from what I could gather, Brawny was requesting that he open it up so he could check for weapons, and the guy was balking. Brawny was insisting loudly enough that I could almost hear his words over the sound of the music.

The man in black suddenly turned from Brawny, dismissing him entirely, and looked my way.

There was a little light on Brawny's tiny podium that lit the man's face enough for me to recognize him as the man I knew as Joshua Satterfield.

CHAPTER 29

THINGS happened very quickly after we locked eyes. I reached into my jacket to grab my gun out of its holster. Satterfield just as swiftly reached into his coat and pulled out a butcher knife, which gleamed wickedly in the light from Brawny's station. Brawny started to shout something, but that was as far as he got. Satterfield swung the knife and made a huge gash across Brawny's throat. Blood splattered onto the wall behind Brawny. I fired. I thought I hit Satterfield, but if I did, he didn't react. He moved fast. I expected him to go for the door, where he'd just entered, but instead he darted further into the bar, making for the shadows at the end furthest from the bar. I fired again.

People began screaming and running. There was a mass exodus for the door, putting people in between me and Satterfield. The guy I had pegged as a plainclothes cop pulled out his gun. He was closer to Satterfield than I was. Too close as it turned out. Before he could bring his weapon up Satterfield was on him. He rammed the knife into the man's chest. The cop gasped and convulsed. I saw blood coming out of his mouth before he hit the floor.

I couldn't imagine what Satterfield had in mind until I saw that one of the girls was sitting at a corner table having a smoke break. She was still wearing her stiletto heels but had a terry cloth robe on, covering her stripping garb. Her screams were adding to the already ear-splitting din, but she was trapped, cornered.

Jesus, I thought. Satterfield was getting bold. He'd decided on getting his meal tonight, and he'd decided on his favorite spot, and he wasn't going to let me, Brawny, or the police stop him. I got a clear shot and fired again. Either I was missing, which, let's face it, wasn't likely, or bullets really didn't bother him much.

Satterfield was getting close to the girl. She tried to move around him, but he quickly stepped in front of her. He raised the knife.

More than human strength. Silver bullets couldn't kill him. He was armed with a butcher knife and had just either killed or seriously wounded two people right in front of me. The only smart thing to do was to get the hell out of there, and let the police try to deal with him.

Not me. I bolted across the room and threw myself at him.

I slammed into his back, shoulder first, with everything I had. This didn't have the effect that I'd hoped. Instead of tumbling to the ground he merely lost his balance momentarily. It did give the stripper enough time to get away from him, though. She let out one last blood-curdler and, ducking out of range of his knife, managed to squeeze around us. She moved fast for someone in stiletto heels.

Satterfield, or whatever the ghoul's real name was, moved fast as well. With an angry snarl he whirled around, slashing the knife at me. My flying tackle had put me off balance as well and, more by luck than design, I missed getting sliced because I was already falling back on my ass. Satterfield growled with rage and brought the knife back around. This time he nicked my jacket. This guy was murder on jackets. I didn't think that he'd cut me, but I didn't stay still to examine any possible wounds. I scrambled away just in time. I could feel the rush of the air as the knife swished right by my ear. I kicked back blindly and managed to connect with one of his shins. I heard him grunt, but I think it was more out of frustration than out of pain. To him I was a pesky fly that refused to sit still long enough to be hit with the swatter.

I got to my feet and grabbed the nearest chair. I could sense more than see him moving behind me. I swung the chair around just as he was making a try to stab me in the chest. The legs of the chair hit his descending arm and sent the knife flying. His eyes flashed anger, but before he could react, I swung the chair back around, this time making sure it collided with his shoulder.

He fell back, hitting the table where the girl had been taking her break. The table kept him from falling over, damn the luck. He spun around, glaring at me. "I'm going to kill you," he snarled through clenched teeth.

"That's hardly pithy or original," I yelled as I crashed the chair onto his head. Unlike in the movies, it didn't splinter into pieces. I heard some wood crack, but that was it. The force pushed him farther back, and he and the table went over.

I knew he was only stunned, but I'd saved my damsel in distress. Now it was time to get the hell away from him. I turned and started to run. That's when I realized we weren't the only ones left in the bar. When the commotion had started all the staff and patrons had taken off running. All but three, apparently. Cowering over by the bar were Tiffany, Craig, and Brenda.

I wondered why the hell they were hanging around until I got a better look at Tiffany, who was sprawled on the floor, cradled by her brother. He and Brenda were trying to get her to her feet. It wasn't easy because Tiffany's leg was broken. Badly. Even from several yards away I could see her shin bone poking through the skin. She must have fallen off the bar when the panic started.

I rushed over and got on the side of her that was opposite Craig. Together we got her to her feet. Satterfield was moving as well, and I knew there was no way we could drag Tiffany to the main door without Satterfield catching up with us.

"This way," I shouted. I started for the door I'd seen Brenda go through when she went to change. Together Craig and I dragged his sister quickly across the floor, Brenda close on our heels. We got there just in time. Once we were through, Brenda slammed the door behind us. There was a bolt on the door, and just as she slid it across, the door shook as Satterfield rammed into it. It held, but it wouldn't take much abuse. I quickly took stock. Tiffany couldn't walk and was a bawling, screaming mess in any case. Not that you could blame her. Brenda was wearing nothing but a pink G-string and heels, so running quickly wasn't going to be easy for her.

"Is there a back door?" I asked.

Brenda nodded. She was choking back tears, but she was thinking. Satterfield hit the door again, and this time I heard wood splintering. The lock wasn't going to last long. I scooped Tiffany into my arms. She put an arm around my neck. She wasn't too heavy, and I figured I could move faster like that than trying to carry her with help from Craig.

I wouldn't say things looked good for us. Brenda was having difficulty running in her heels, and her breasts bounced around enough to provide difficulties of their own. I had the nearly-naked Tiffany in my arms. Brenda led the way to the back door. Just as we got there I heard a crashing and more splintering of wood. Satterfield had broken through the door.

We wasted no time getting outside. There was no way to lock the outside door behind us. Craig, pulling up the rear, paused long enough to grab a table lamp and hurl it toward Satterfield before slamming the door behind us. Hopefully he slowed down Satterfield a few seconds. We needed all the help we could get.

I sprinted around the side of the building to the parking lot. Robbie was waiting by the car, his face tense and alert. He quickly rushed around and opened up the back door. Tiffany was moaning, and her face was looking pasty and feverish.

I noticed that the cop who had been in the patrol car was no longer there. He had either heard the commotion inside or been alerted when the staff and patrons had all run out. I couldn't see him anywhere, and I guessed that he had gone inside to see what was up. I hoped that he had had the sense to call for backup.

Craig motioned to a car that was actually closer than mine. "Put her in the back seat," he told me. Must be his car. I got to the car at the same time as Craig, and he opened the back door. I didn't have time to be gentle, and Tiffany cried out when her damaged leg brushed up against the car door. Somehow I got her in. Craig opened the passenger door and got inside and then slid across to the driver's seat. I shut Tiffany in and glanced back. Satterfield was only yards behind us. There was no way Brenda and I were going to be able to get inside before he'd reach us.

A gunshot rang out and Satterfield stumbled. Behind him was the patrol cop, who must have followed us out the back door. He fired again, and Satterfield fell face forward onto the pavement.

Before he recovered Craig gunned the engine. His tires spun as he punched the accelerator before sending the car careening across the parking lot. I saw that the cop was running up to Satterfield, who was slowly getting back up to his feet. He shot Satterfield one more time. Satterfield's body jerked from the impact.

"Don't come close to him," I warned the cop. "Bullets can't kill him."

Craig didn't even try to aim for the entrance to the parking lot. He ran over the curb, sending sparks flying. The tires squealed as he sped away.

Brenda watched the tail lights as they headed down the road. "He left us," she wailed.

"Get in my car," I told her as I ran over to where Satterfield was once again rising from the pavement. I got to him at the same time as the cop, who still had his gun out.

He was watching Satterfield get up in astonishment. "I put three bullets in his back!"

I had the idea that if I could get the amulet from around the killer's neck that maybe the gun would become an effective weapon. No charm, no powers. He recovered quickly, though. He whirled around to the cop, who was too close to him. Satterfield's left hand shot out and grabbed the officer by the throat. The cop dropped his gun as he raised his hands to try to pry away the fingers that were squeezing his windpipe. I got to Satterfield, but he must have seen me out of the corner of his eye. He was holding the cop with one hand. He used his other to backhand me. I didn't see it coming, and his fist hit me right in the mouth with considerable power. I hit the ground, feeling blood in my mouth. My lip was cut badly. That wouldn't look good while it healed.

Satterfield raised the cop off the ground, still using only his left hand. The cop struggled for air and kicked his legs. Then something in his neck snapped, and his head lolled to the side, his eyes staring and his tongue bulging out of his mouth. Satterfield tossed him aside as if he were a rag doll.

I got to my feet and moved away from the ghoul. I wouldn't be able to get to the amulet, and trying would only get me killed. Then he would go after Brenda and kill her, and that would make me a very bad protector. I'd also be dead, but that was secondary to being a bad protector. I had to get Brenda away from him. That's what I was being paid to do.

I got around and got into the car. Robbie was in his usual place and Brenda had gotten into the back. Just as I shut my door Satterfield reached the car. I got the key in the ignition and fired up the engine. The back window shattered as Satterfield rammed his fist through it. Brenda screamed as his hand reached in, trying to grasp her hair. The car shot forward and Satterfield got his hand out just in time. We sped away, leaving him looking very angry indeed. I got an idea in my head of going back and running him over with the car. Surely that would do some damage. When I glanced back in the rear view mirror, though, Satterfield was gone. The man could move fast for a guy a couple of centuries old.

"What the hell?" Robbie asked. He was twisted in his seat, trying to see out the rear window.

"Did you see where he went?" I asked as I rounded a corner. The tires squealed in protest.

Robbie shook his head. "He must have disappeared into the shadows. What happened in there?"

Brenda was crying, the sobs wracking her body. The glass from the broken window lay around her and there was even some in her hair, but I couldn't see that she was cut anywhere. I slowed the car down a little. We were heading down 16th Street and had passed the

Indianapolis Speedway at a speed that wouldn't have been out of place on the track. Robbie turned to face the front as I told him, "Not much. Our ghoul apparently came in thinking he'd have a quick murder and a snack later. I saw him. He saw me. Death and destruction all around."

Several patrol cars zoomed by us, their lights flashing and sirens wailing. They paid us no attention. I could hear sirens coming from somewhere behind us as well. The force had arrived, although I wondered if they'd find Satterfield still there. It was hard to tell what the ghoul would do, but I didn't think he'd be stupid enough to hang around after all that. Of course, I hadn't thought he'd be stupid enough to walk into a strip club carrying his knife. Well, I say stupid. I was the one with the busted lip.

CHAPTER 30

I WANTED to head straight for the nearest police station, but Brenda vetoed me, pleading in a loud and choked voice that she wanted to go home to Derek. We were headed in that direction so I gave in. I could drop her off and then check in with Lieutenant Carson or whoever was around that I knew and see if there was anything I could do. Traffic was light since it was still the wee hours and the middle of the week. We made good time downtown and were soon pulling into the parking garage of the Whitcomb Towers Apartments. Before we got out of the car, I took off my jacket and handed it back for Brenda to wear. If we ran across any of her new neighbors on the way up to the twentieth floor I didn't want them to see her mostly naked. They might not approve. Or they might approve too much, which could bring another set of problems.

We took the connecting hall that led to the apartment building itself. Brenda was holding my jacket tightly closed as she scooted along in her heels. "What do you think happened to Tiff and Craig?"

"I imagine he headed for the nearest hospital," I said. "You can call Methodist, if you like. I imagine that's where they went."

We passed a guy coming out of the elevators. His eyes bugged as he caught sight of us, looking first at me, then for a longer time at Brenda, and finally at Robbie. I don't know how clearly he could see Robbie, but the guy's expression was enough to show that he knew someone was there. He moved faster as he walked away from us, glancing back twice while we trundled into the elevator car.

When Derek opened the door he looked weary at first. Then he got a good look at us, and he gasped. Pulling Brenda into a hug, he asked, "What happened? Oh, my God, are you all right?"

Brenda's tears began flowing again. I had thought she was all cried out, but apparently she had some reserves. She couldn't answer, so I did. "We ran into a little trouble." We went inside, and I briefly recounted our night. Derek's grip on his wife tightened as he listened.

"Holy shit," was his only comment.

Robbie walked into the living room. It was all a jumble of boxes and packing materials but there was a couch, some chairs, and a big plasma television that had already been hooked up. It wasn't on. The furniture I assumed was a gift from Ma Sanderson. I couldn't imagine that it was purchased on Derek's junkyard money. It could have been paid for by Brenda, I supposed, but that would have been a lot of stuffed dollar bills and lap dances. I looked around for a phone. The battery on my cell was dead. There was one on a small table by the couch. "Mind if I make a call?"

Derek nodded. Brenda's face was buried in his chest. Robbie was wandering around aimlessly. The sliding glass door leading to the balcony was open, making the living room a little too cool. A new grill was sitting out there, having been newly assembled. That had obviously been what Derek had been working on when we arrived. Robbie sauntered out onto the balcony as I dialed.

Before I completed the number, though, my blood froze. Seconds later there was a quiet knock at the door. Not good. Satterfield had followed us. I had been in such a hurry to get away that I hadn't even bothered to take a more circuitous route to the Whitcomb. There hadn't been much traffic, and I didn't notice anyone behind us, but it wouldn't have been hard to follow our taillights. Satterfield obviously had. I must have really pissed him off.

"Don't answer that!" I shouted.

I didn't get it out in time. Derek had disengaged himself from Brenda and had already turned the knob before I got my warning out.

The door was shoved open, and Derek grunted as Satterfield plunged his butcher knife into the boy's gut. Brenda screamed. There was a sick, wet sound as Satterfield twisted the knife before pulling it back out of Derek's body. The blade shone with dark red blood. I saw Derek's eyes as he fell to the floor. The boy was dead before he hit.

I dropped the phone and threw myself at Satterfield, making sure to keep myself between him and Brenda. He swung the knife, and he cut me across the right bicep. I felt the sting of the blade, but I couldn't tell how bad he got me. I lashed out with my left and hit him across the cheek. Robbie had come back into the room and had picked up a flower pot. Weirdly, my mind registered that the flowers were plastic as he hurled the pot at Satterfield. It hit the ghoul in the face but had as much effect as my punch, which wasn't much. Brenda continued to scream but instead of running into the bedroom and locking herself in, she went for the balcony. Satterfield pushed me aside and went after her.

I got up in time to see Satterfield cornering Brenda at the railing of the balcony. He raised the knife. I ran and leaped onto the ghoul's back, grabbing at his upraised hand as best I could with my damaged arm. Brenda screamed again and moved just in time. I'd hit Satterfield with enough force that he tumbled forward. We both went over the rail. If Brenda hadn't moved in time, she'd have gone with us.

My adrenaline was pumping enough that time seemed to be slowed down. I saw something flash in the moonlight and realized that Satterfield's amulet had come out of his shirt. I grabbed hold of the railing with my right hand and reached out with my left. Satterfield was tumbling in the air, but somehow I grabbed the amulet. I felt the leather strap snap as he fell away from me. The hand not holding the knife made a last, desperate grab at me but not in time. He fell twenty floors.

I was about to join him. I was hanging in the air, holding on to the rail with a cut arm that was gushing blood. What little strength the arm possessed was giving out. I couldn't haul myself up.

Then a hand grabbed hold of my wrist. Robbie. His face was a study in concentration as he willed himself solid enough to hold on to me. I could even feel him pull. "Come on," he yelled down at me. "Work with me here!"

I gritted my teeth. "I'm trying!"

"Try harder!" I could see sweat breaking out on his forehead. He was using everything he had just to hold me there. I tried to move but my arm gave out. My fingers let go of the rail. If Robbie hadn't been holding on, I'd have joined Satterfield on the Super Express Elevator going straight down to the pavement. Robbie pulled. I got hold of the rail again and got my left, good arm up. It was still clutching the amulet. I let it fall onto the balcony and grasped hold of the railing. Robbie pulled harder. I'd never known him to exert so much energy. "I'm not letting you go," he said.

"I appreciate that!" I said. Poor guy. He was giving it all he had. I could see his image start to fade. I had to say something, just in case I didn't make it back over the rail. "I love you," I said.

"Good!" Robbie shouted. "Prove it by pulling yourself back up here!"

I strained every muscle in my arms. Robbie was nearly transparent now. He was just a black and white figure that was there, but not there. He gave one last yank as I put everything I had into one last effort. I went up and over the rail. I felt one of Robbie's hands gripping the collar of my shirt, getting me the rest of the way over the railing. I tumbled over just as he vanished completely. He was gone. I couldn't even get a sense of him.

Brenda knelt down to see that I was okay, but then she remembered Derek. There was hurt and anguish in her eyes as she went back inside to him. I got to my feet to see her huddled over by the door, cradling him against her. Her cries were gut-wrenching.

I looked over the rail. Satterfield had hit the sidewalk leading up to the main door of the apartment building. There was no body, however. Just bones and the clothes he'd been wearing, fluttering slightly in the breeze.

I held my arm and went back inside. I was losing a lot of blood, and now that everything was over, it was beginning to smart like hell. Picking up the phone, I dialed 911 while listening to Brenda's anguished wailing. I couldn't blame her. She'd lost the man she loved, due to my stupidity really, and for all I knew I'd lost the man I loved as well. Something felt empty inside me. I hadn't felt that empty since Robbie had first died. Somehow I felt that he'd used so much energy that there was nothing left. I'd never see him again.

CHAPTER 31

GINA handed Lieutenant Carson a cup of tea. "It's my own blend. I hope you like it."

Carson acted like he didn't want to touch the cup and saucer. He bit his lip. "It's not anything... weird, is it?" He didn't know Gina was a witch, but I guess her friendship with me made her suspect.

Smiling, Gina said, "Only if you find peppermint weird."

Carson was dubious, but he took a sip. His face cleared of anxiety, and he nodded to Gina. "It's very good."

It had been several days since I'd performed my circus act on the balcony twenty floors up. My left arm was in a sling and had been nicely stitched up. The cut had been deep but hadn't done any irreparable muscle damage. Gina would ensure that I'd heal.

We were in my living room. Carson had "dropped by" just to see how I was doing, but I knew he wanted some answers, even if they couldn't be put into the official police report. The amulet was sitting on the coffee table in front of him. Every now and then he glanced at it as if it were a snake about to pounce.

Of Robbie, there was no sign. I couldn't feel his presence in the apartment. Gina and I had hoped that he'd show back up in the place where he felt most comfortable, but as the days went by it felt less and less likely. Gina had even tried to read her Tarot cards and looked into her crystal ball. No sign of him anywhere. She tried to be hopeful when she was around me, but I could see in her eyes that she didn't believe I'd see him again. He'd used all his earthly energy to save me.

Carson had some more tea. "Officially the case is closed. I'm sure you've seen some of it on the news."

I had. A police shootout in the parking lot of Pickin's had resulted in a chase that had ended up at the Whitcomb Apartments. Several people had been killed, including an employee at Pickin's, two police officers, one Derek Schneider, and a man who'd been using the name Joshua Satterfield. Real name unknown. The last victim was believed to be the man who had also murdered three local strippers. I stopped watching the news after a few such reports.

I was sitting in an armchair opposite Carson. Gina took a seat on the couch with Carson. Daisy hopped up between them and gave Carson's hand a lick. Carson's mouth twitched.

"Your dog looks weird. What's wrong with her eyes?"

"Do you really want to know?" I asked.

He shook his head wearily. "I wish I didn't even know you. Every time you show up in a case suddenly nothing makes sense. We have some bones at the morgue that the medical examiner says are several hundred years old."

"Odd I didn't see anything about that on the news."

"You won't, either. As far as the public is concerned, we have a regular body. He was the killer, and he fell to his death. Case closed." He nudged the coffee table with his foot, unwilling to actually come into contact with the amulet. "And then there's this thing."

"You can touch it," Gina said. "It's completely harmless now. It's been damaged, and the magical properties it held are no longer."

"Magic." Carson snorted. "I shouldn't even be listening to such nonsense."

Gina's eyes twinkled. "But that's just it, isn't it? You know it isn't nonsense."

Carson grunted and drank some more of Gina's tea. He cocked an eyebrow at her. "This really is good tea." Setting the tea aside, he leaned forward and examined the amulet. Still attached to the broken leather strap, the amulet looked to be a heart-sized piece of carved wood. In the center was a black gemstone. Around the stone several shapes, including lightning bolts and a quarter moon, were carved. Some of the shapes had become so worn over the years that it was hard to decide what they were meant to depict. "So this kept our killer alive for several hundred years."

"Apparently," I said.

"Any idea what it is or was?"

Gina nodded. "I believe that it was the Pendant of Asmodeus."

Caron blinked. "Asmo-who?"

"Asmodeus. In *The Book of Tobit*, which is part of the Catholic Bible, Asmodeus was a jealous demon who killed every man who married a woman named Sarah. Asmodeus loved Sarah himself, so every time she got married the demon murdered her husband on the wedding night before the marriage could be consummated."

"Nice guy," Carson said.

"Asmodeus killed seven of Sarah's husbands until God sent the angel Raphael, disguised as a human, to rid Sarah of this demon."

"Uh-huh," Carson said slowly. It was all a bit beyond him. It was a bit beyond me as well, to be honest.

"There's always been a legend that something of Asmodeus survived. A piece of his heart was supposed to have been put into a stone, and that stone was set into a wood carving." She picked up the amulet and shook it under Carson's nose. "Anyone who wore the amulet would be protected from death. They would never die."

"It didn't seem to work for this guy," Carson said.

"He wasn't wearing it when he fell," Gina reminded him. "The amulet was damaged even before that, though. It was losing its magic. The carvings were becoming too worn. Our ghoul must have come across the amulet a couple of hundred years ago. It made him almost human and very nearly immortal."

"As long as he kept eating bits of people." Carson finished his tea with a satisfied look. Without asking Gina got up and went to the kitchen to get the pot. She refilled his cup and Carson beamed thanks at her.

"Only every hundred years. And he only had to kill seven people and eat one of their organs. For a ghoul, that's being frugal."

"A ghoul." Carson scratched his cheek. "And just what is a ghoul, anyway? I always thought the word referred to grave robbers."

I felt the need to talk. Sitting there not saying anything was making me think of Robbie, and I didn't want to do that. So I said, "As Gina explained it to me, real ghouls are all but extinct. Our killer may have been the last of his kind. Ghouls are demons who eat the dead. Usually they then take on the shape of the person they just ate, but our friend seems to have found a way around that. The amulet probably kept him from changing shape if he didn't want to. I think it's significant that he always killed seven people to eat every hundred years."

Carson gave me a blank stare.

"In 1810 seven showgirls were murdered in Stockholm. In 1910 he re-surfaced in Springfield, Illinois. Again seven showgirls were killed."

"Why seven?" Carson asked. "What's the significance?"

Gina shrugged. "Asmodeus murdered seven of Sarah's husbands. The number of deaths was set into the stone that became part of the amulet."

"But why showgirls? This Asmodeus killed husbands, not girls who shook their booty."

"The choice of victims, I'm sure, was entirely up to whoever wore the amulet," Gina replied. "We'll probably never know why he chose strippers and showgirls. Maybe our ghoul had a hatred of showgirls."

"Or maybe the opposite," I offered. "Maybe he liked them. A lot. Liked them enough to eat."

Carson gingerly took the amulet from Gina's hands. When it didn't bite him, he turned it around and examined it carefully. "It doesn't look powerful."

"It isn't," Gina said. "Not now."

My arm itched. I shifted it around in the sling, hoping that would help. It didn't. "You can have that if you want, Lieutenant."

Carson chuckled and tossed the amulet back onto the coffee table. "For what? Evidence? I don't think so. No, this thing stays with you. You can keep it. Years from now it will remind you of these last few weeks."

Like I could ever forget. I looked around the room. It felt so empty. So did I.

THE following Monday, at Janice Sanderson's request, I once again took the long trek down her driveway. Thanks to Gina my arm was no longer in a sling, but it was still stiff and a little painful. It didn't hamper my driving, thankfully. I parked and got out of the car, pausing before going up to the door. I looked at the house. It seemed to be looking back at me. I didn't want to go inside, but Janice had wanted to give me her check in person. "So I can properly thank you," she had said over the phone.

I had, it was true, managed to save her daughter from becoming a victim of the ghoul. Brenda's husband had died in her arms, though, and I felt responsible for that death. There should have been something I could have done. He'd been a nice kid, despite the fact that he'd punched me when we first met. He didn't deserve to die like that.

Janice had told me that Brenda was staying with her for the time being. "She doesn't want to live in that apartment," Janice had said.

Who could blame her?

I sighed and went up the steps and rang the bell. After a few moments the door was opened by Brenda. She looked pale and there were circles under her eyes. She tried to smile at me and failed at the attempt. "Come in," she said.

I went in. She shut the door and attempted the smile again. This time she almost made it. "Your arm is better," she said.

"Gina works wonders," I replied.

Brenda nodded. "I remember." She sniffed and looked like she wanted to say something else. I waited. Finally she said, "Derek's funeral is Wednesday. I'd really like it if you could come."

"I'll be there," I promised.

She ran a hand through her hair. "I look like shit, don't I? I don't think I've slept for days." She looked in the direction of the living room. "Mother's been pretty good about it all. She's even said some nice things about Derek. I was afraid she'd gloat or tell me I was better off with him dead."

Even Ma Sanderson wouldn't be that cruel. The thought brought tears to Brenda's eyes. She looked like she needed a hug, so I put my arms around her. She sobbed and rested her head against my chest.

"I miss him so much," she said.

"I know."

We stood there while she cried herself out. Then she stood back and wiped her eyes. "I think I'm ready for a nap. Mom's in the living room."

"I know the way," I said.

Brenda nodded. "I keep on dreaming he's still alive. Sometimes I even think he's still alive when I'm awake. Then I remember."

I knew what she was going through. I'd been there. Hell, I was there again. I was in the same spot. I'd wake up, thinking Robbie was in the room. Then I'd remember. I had no words of comfort, so I changed the subject. "I talked to Craig yesterday. Tiffany is doing just fine. She hates the cast and the crutches, but she's getting around. It'll be quite a while before she can start working, though."

That got me a genuine smile. "I can't believe they just left us."

"There was a lot of crazy shit happening. Don't think too badly of Craig. He was looking after his sister."

"He left us to be killed by that maniac."

"Okay, you can think badly of him a little." I reached out and stroked Brenda's cheek. She seemed appreciative of the gesture. "What are you going to do?" I asked her.

She shook her head. "I'm not sure. I can't live here. That's for sure. Once everything settles down, I'll look for an apartment somewhere. Get a job."

"You're not going back to Pickin's?"

"No. I couldn't. Too many memories. Besides, I think that was just me being rebellious. And I'm not feeling too rebellious right now." Once again her eyes filled with tears. "I hadn't planned on falling in love."

"None of us do."

Brenda embraced me again. "Thanks for saving my life," she said.

"Anytime."

She ran a hand over her cheeks to wipe away the rivulets and then gave me a little wave of farewell. She walked slowly up the stairs, and I made my way into the living room to face her mother.

Ma Sanderson was wearing a simple black dress. She may not have liked the idea of her daughter being married to trailer trash like Derek Schneider, but she at least was showing respect by mourning. She rose to greet me and extended her hand. I shook it.

"I have a check for you," she said.

"You could have mailed it."

Janice Sanderson nodded and offered me a seat. We sat. She regarded me carefully. "I wasn't really sure why I asked you to watch after my daughter. I didn't really think she'd be in danger from that man, that killer. The possibility seemed so… remote." She brushed some imaginary lint from the arm of the chair she sat in. "I think I really just wanted to show Brenda that I was watching out for her. That I cared."

I didn't say anything. There wasn't anything to say.

Janice reached over to the small table next to her chair and picked up a check. She'd already filled it out. Handing it to me, she said, "I want to thank you for saving her life. You're quite a remarkable man, Mr. Duncan Andrews."

I didn't feel remarkable. The check was nice, though. It was for quite a bit more than I'd told her.

"I added a bonus," she said, reading my mind. "I don't really know what happened that night. Brenda doesn't say much, and the reports on the news didn't make any sense. They make it sound like the police shot the killer, and he fell off the balcony, but I know that's not what happened. Brenda told me there were no police there. Just you."

Just me, Brenda, Derek, a ghost named Robbie, and a ghoul. Only Brenda and I had survived. Not really a victory. I put the check in my top pocket and rose. "Thank you," I said. She started to rise, but I told her I could show myself out.

I got to the door but stopped when I heard thundering footsteps on the stairs behind me. I turned to see Kevin Sanderson rushing toward me. He was a little out of breath and nearly didn't stop in time, missing colliding with me by centimeters. "Mr. Andrews!" he said.

I smiled at him. He seemed taller than the first time I'd seen him. Maybe he was just standing straighter. "Kevin," I said.

"I wanted to thank you again for the tickets."

"My pleasure. Have you found someone to take?"

He nodded. "I think I'm going to take my sister. She needs

cheering up. She likes the Jonas Brothers, too, even though she doesn't want people to know."

I ruffled the kid's hair. "I think taking your sister would be a good idea."

Kevin stuck out his hand for me to shake. It was a firm, businesslike handshake. "I'll look after her," he told me.

"She's in good hands, then."

TUESDAY night there was a knock at my door. Daisy barked out a warning but became all love and slobber when I opened the door to find Nick there. He kissed me briefly on the cheek before kneeling down to give attention to Daisy. She rolled over onto her belly as he patted her.

"I wasn't expecting you," I said. Nick had called over the weekend, and I'd filled him in on some of the details, but we hadn't seen each other all week. I was glad he was here, though.

"I was in the neighborhood," he said. We both knew it was a lie, but we let it go. We sat down next to each other on the couch. Our arms were nearly but not quite touching. He looked at the stitched wound on my other arm. "That looks nasty."

"You should have seen it days ago," I told him.

He nodded and looked around the apartment. He seemed very uncomfortable. "So… still no Robbie."

"No Robbie."

"Do you think—?"

I stopped him. "I don't dare think. I have to believe he'll be back. I don't think I could go on without him." For the first time since he disappeared, the thought of Robbie made me smile. "He was such a funny kid. You know he even had a plan to ask you if you'd agree to let him possess you for a short time so that we could have sex again."

Nick looked alarmed but intrigued. "Really? That's… that's weird."

"Desperation makes you weird. He saw it as something worth pursuing."

Nick pondered the thought. "It would be kind of like a threesome, wouldn't it? In a strange kind of way."

"In a strange kind of way," I agreed.

Shrugging, Nick said, "I'd at least have given it some thought."

"Really?"

He nodded. "I'd have considered it, anyway. You two really loved each other."

"We did." I hated using the past tense. It was like admitting that Robbie was gone for good.

"So where does this leave us?" Nick looked into my eyes.

"I like you," I said. "I'd still like to see you."

He nodded again. "I'd still like to see you too." He turned and kissed me on the lips. It was a good kiss, but it still made me feel sadder than ever. This was going to take some time. Nick sensed my discomfort and broke away. "I'd better go," he said.

This time I nodded. There was so much to say, and yet no words to say it. Nick rose.

"Want to go out Friday night?" I asked.

He smiled. "I'd like that."

I showed him to the door, and we kissed again, briefly this time. "See ya," I said.

He patted Daisy again and left.

I suddenly felt tired and more drained than I'd been in ages. A shower sounded good, so I went to the bathroom and pulled off my clothes. I made sure the water was as hot as I could stand. That would surely relax my aching muscles, and I'd be able to sleep. I got out and began to dry myself. I was gently patting my wounded arm when I looked over and saw the bathroom mirror. It had steamed up and no reflection could be seen. There were words written in the misty residue.

Very weak. See you soon. Love you, Robbie.

I nearly fell over. I touched the mirror to make sure I wasn't seeing things. I scraped a finger over the V. It was really there. I dropped the towel and looked around the little room, letting my senses seek out every little nook and cranny. I could almost, almost, almost, almost feel him. He was there. Weaker than I'd ever known, but there.

"I love you too," I told the air.

STEPHEN OSBORNE has been an improvisational comedian, a pizza restaurant manager, and a bookseller. Other than writing, his addictions include British television shows, reading mysteries, and (a recent addition) Broadway musicals. He lives in rural Illinois with Jadzia the One-Eyed Wonder Dog.

Visit him at Facebook: http://facebook.com/stephen.osborne2 and Twitter: http://twitter.com/southbendghosts. You can contact him at leftyIN@yahoo.com.